Rev. Jimmy

AN ACT OF FRUSTRATION

To Rev. Jimmy —

Could This happen?

By
Ken Beckley

Ken Beckley

© 2016 Ken Beckley

All Rights Reserved.

No part of this publication may be reproduced, stored in a retrieval system, or transmitted, in any form or by any means, electronic, mechanical, photocopying, recording, or otherwise, without the written permission of the author.

First published by Dog Ear Publishing
4011 Vincennes Rd
Indianapolis, IN 46268
www.dogearpublishing.net

ISBN: 978-1-4575-4543-6

This book is printed on acid-free paper.

This book is a work of fiction. Places, events, and situations in this book are purely fictional and any resemblance to actual persons, living or dead, is coincidental.

Printed in the United States of America

DEDICATION

I dedicate this novel to the memory of Anne B. Kraege, a dear friend whose zest for life and service was infectious to all who knew her. Her inspiring comments about my first work of fiction helped lead me to believe I could write another.

ACKNOWLEDGEMENTS

I'm deeply grateful to Dorothy J. Frapwell for reading the original manuscript and to my editor, Laura Lane, a writer based in southern Indiana, for making significant improvements throughout the writing process. Gratitude also goes to Daniel P. Byron, Esq. and John L. Ebling, ACSW, LCSW for their assistance with sections of the story and to author and fellow alumnus Michael Koryta for his important advice.

CHAPTER

1

The movements of the two figures in shadow created by a full moon were precise and premeditated. One remained at the rear of the pickup truck in the carport beside the ranch-style house while the other lay on his back, dug heels into the gravel, and slowly pushed himself under the driver's side. Moments later, he emerged, whispered "It's set," and the pair walked quietly in the dark until they reached their rental car a block away.

★★★★★

A month earlier, Charlie Simpson's frustration had led to an act that would quickly resonate throughout the United States.

"You are invited to a discussion of what we small business owners can do about the inactions of our federal legislators."

Charlie's name will live in American history. His inspired action in 2016 – an invitation – led to the greatest revolution on U.S. soil since the invention of the Internet; the greatest political revolution since the country's fight for independence more than two centuries earlier. The result was not something he imagined would happen. But Charlie Simpson changed America.

And he paid a terrible price while doing so.

A small-town hardware store owner, Charlie never had a strong political thought except for whom he'd cast votes in local, state and federal elections. In fact, he despised politics and had little regard for politicians – a respect that had grown thin among an increasing number of his fellow countrymen in the past decade. Those in national offices failed to acknowledge the degree of disdain, until it was too late.

★★★★★

His life had always been simple, the product of a father who retired after more than forty years as an automobile mechanic and his late mother who worked as a beautician in a two-person parlor until her legs gave out from standing too many hours for too many years. Velma Simpson collapsed suddenly and died one day in the middle of giving a permanent to one of her clients.

Jefferson, Hopewell County, Indiana, was a wholesome place to raise children and live. It was founded July 4, 1827, exactly a year after its namesake, the principal writer of the Declaration of Independence and third U.S. President, died. In 2016, signs at the entrances to the community on the state highway that ran through it stated *Welcome to Jefferson. Population 5,710 plus two grouchy old men.* Until Charlie's aggressive act, the most famous person who'd lived in Hopewell County was neighboring Barclay's knuckleballer Davie Miller who died of a brain aneurysm while pitching in a major league baseball game in 1990. A statue of him had been erected in downtown Barclay, similar, but smaller than the one at the entrance gates to Duval County Stadium, home of the Jacksonville, Florida team in the American League.

Velma and Horace Simpson's son – their only child – was delivered in St. Mary's Hospital at Evansville in 1961. The pregnancy had been difficult, and Velma suffered from abdominal pain off and on for thirty years until she died.

Their ancestry was English/Welsh and the generations before them settled in southwestern Indiana, mostly farming for a living after clearing an abundance of trees from the rolling land that lay about twenty miles north of the Ohio River and fifteen east of the Wabash. The soil was fertile and in most years produced plentiful corn and grain to provide a modest lifestyle. Velma Pembroke grew up on the farm adjacent to the Simpson family.

Horace didn't share his father's love of tilling the earth and harvesting crops but learned enough about repairing and maintaining farm machinery that he found a job as an auto mechanic at Bud's Texaco in Jefferson two years before he and Velma were married.

Charlie was a good child, never causing his parents any problems except for the time he and his pal Jerry Tevault skipped school to attend the Shrine Circus in Evansville. A fellow student's mother saw them at the Friday afternoon matinee and reported it to the Jefferson High School principal. As seniors with spotless behavior records, they were placed on probation for only the next month of the academic year. Horace laughed it off, but Velma displayed her displeasure by grounding her son from any activities the weekend after the event.

The Evansville regional campus of Indiana State University was Charlie's entry into higher education in the fall of 1979. His solid B grade point average in high school was sufficient for acceptance but he had no idea what his major would be. He commuted throughout his freshman year more than forty miles daily to the college on Evansville's west side, then settled into a rental house with three other students the following fall. A nearby fast food restaurant set him on a career path.

A year later – "Anyone sitting here?" he asked, balancing his tray and motioning to a two-person table at Bob's Burgers. "It's all yours," replied the strawberry blonde in an adjacent seat, a cheeseburger and french fries on her plate.

Charlie placed the tray on the table and slid into a seat with his back to the window, facing the stranger he later described to his roommates as "darned cute." He wasn't shy but still not forward enough to begin a conversation, so he began eating his all-too-typical lunch of a Big Bob – two hamburger patties, cheese, onion, and pickle – fries, and a Coke accompanied by several packets of catsup.

She broke the silence. "You go to ISUE?"

He looked up. "Yeah. I'm a sophomore. You?"

"Freshman. Since school started last month I've been trying to get used to it but it seems all I do is study."

"Where you from?"

"Holland."

"Wow, must be a big adjustment coming to the U.S. and entering college all at the same time."

She laughed. "Oh, no. I meant Holland, Indiana, about fifty miles from here."

He chuckled. "Sorry. I made a quick assumption. Actually, I've heard of your Holland but I don't know anything about it."

"It's a little town. Our claim to fame is Holland Dairy."

"You're kidding! I didn't know it was located there. I've been drinking Holland milk all my life. Never gave a thought as to where it was produced. Must be the most popular milk in southern Indiana."

"Well, I don't know about that, but it's pretty big."

"What's your major?"

"I think art history or art education, at least that's what I'm leaning toward. I've always had an interest since a high school field trip to the Evansville Museum of Art. Yours?"

"Still undecided. I'm struggling with what a career path might be. Maybe something to do with business."

"I've been told not to worry about or get obsessed with what a person majors in. More important to get a degree of some type. Besides, you still have 'til the end of this year to declare, don't you?"

"Yeah. And it'll take 'til then, the way I'm going."

She held out her hand across the table. "I'm Sarah. Sarah Carter."

"Charlie. Charlie Simpson," returning the gesture and producing a slight smile. "I'm from Jefferson."

"Jefferson! That's a big city!"

"Naw, less than six thousand, I think."

"Well, when you're from Holland everything seems big. I think our town's only about 700." She paused. "I went to Southridge High School and I think we played Jefferson in basketball."

"Must have been last year when I was here at ISUE. I didn't play ball, but went to games when I was in high school and I know we didn't play Southridge then."

"I could be mistaken but I'm pretty sure we did. We probably got beat since Jefferson's such a big city."

Neither continued the conversation. Charlie looked at his food and resumed eating, not knowing what else to talk about. Cautiously, he raised his eyes, saw Sarah toying with her fries and catsup, and had the feeling she seemed to want to say more. But didn't.

Minutes passed, Charlie, always a quick eater, finished his meal, slid out of the seat, picked up his tray, and started to walk toward the exit. But he paused. "Nice to meet you, Sarah. I'm sure I'll see you around campus. It's not that big."

"Nice to meet you, too, Charlie," she smiled, and they held eyes for a moment, until he spoke.

"Be careful on campus with your wooden shoes."

Sarah cast a quizzical look, a frown. Then they both burst out laughing. Charlie turned and headed to the door.

It was the first time he'd ever felt anything special about a girl, if only for a fleeting moment.

The restaurant manager approached as Charlie was clearing items from his tray near the exit. "Just a reminder that you're on all weekend."

"Yeah, no problem. I'll be here after class Friday afternoon."

★★★★★

Charlie wasn't in love with working at Bob's and the small hourly wage he earned, but it helped his parents pay for college. Work was not foreign to him. Each summer between high school years, he earned money helping farmers detassel corn and bale hay and straw. A job picking peaches at Lynn Orchard near Jefferson lasted but one week. Peach fuzz that found its way down under the back neck of his shirt drove him crazy on hot, humid days, so much that he informed his parents he would never return to the job even if they whipped him for days. It was just an expression. Horace and Velma would never lay a hand on him.

Charlie started the job as a cook at Bob's Burgers the week before fall classes began his sophomore year. His insistence on store cleanliness later in life came from the experience. "Work areas and public areas must be spotless at all times. Your work clothing must be spotless at the beginning of your shift; no exceptions," manager Dick Saunders instructed the day Charlie was hired. "We'll provide two uniforms for you. We expect groomed hair, well-maintained facial hair if you grow any, and absolutely clean hands and fingernails at all times. Also, no facial jewelry and that includes ears, eyebrows, nose, lips and tongue. And if you can think of someplace else to place it on your head, just tempt me. No exceptions. Got it?" Charlie surmised Saunders was in his early thirties and a little gruff for someone in management, but that was just an initial impression. He knew he'd learn more from and about the manager and his style as time went on. "Got it," Charlie responded.

In taking the job, Charlie intended to absorb everything he could about management and personnel and about customers and their whims. He met owner Bob Ringham the day he applied for the job and was impressed with the man's kindness, attention to detail and philosophies about customer service and restaurant cleanliness. It was Ringham's only restaurant and he opened it in 1976 to take advantage of the nearby students, faculty, and staff. Saunders was the lead manager and Charlie knew he was only carrying out what Ringham required, although Charlie felt there could be less edge to Saunder's voice.

Business Management was the academic path he decided on during the middle of the spring semester that year. He thought he'd like to have his own company someday, although what it would be didn't occupy even a speck in his brain. He just knew he didn't want to spend his life working "for the other guy." "Your life is not your own," he told Horace one day when they were discussing his possible future. "You know that, from having worked for Bud for so long." Charlie was careful not to belittle his father, whom he loved, or disrespectful of his dad's employer at the service station.

"I just know that if you work for someone else, they can fire you for almost no reason at all or they can decide to reduce their staff," Charlie continued. "And I've heard of more and more companies terminating people at about the time they reach 55 or 60, saying it was for financial reasons. In one of my classes we talked about Indiana's 'employment at will' law, meaning the will of the company. For practically no reason other than some sort of discrimination, you can be fired."

"But I've always believed, and tried to tell you, that if you give your best effort every minute on the job and have a great attitude, you'll be okay," Horace responded.

"Well, that's not good enough for me," Charlie said. "I agree with the hard work and attitude but I'm not going to trust my future to someone who cares more about making money than his employees. I'd at least like to try it on my own someday."

Horace and Velma had graduated from Jefferson High School but never sought further formal education. He admired his son and listened intently to everything he said, even if he didn't agree with all of it. He knew Charlie had a lot to learn about life.

"I certainly understand, Charlie. There've been times I wished I had my own station but there's a huge financial risk with being your own boss and I never felt confident enough I could pull it off."

Charlie noticed his dad's hair had acquired more gray than he'd recalled from just a few years earlier and his thick, rugged hands were those of a man who'd worked on cars and pickups all his life. Horace's fingernails and finger tips always had a dark greasy appearance despite all the Goop hand cleaner he used. But Charlie admired his father more than he'd ever shared and found him always upbeat, regardless of whatever challenges he and Velma had in their lives. They were a church-going, God-fearing couple who raised Charlie to respect others, be kind, and believe in himself. As early as junior high, they stressed the importance of a college degree. By the time he was a high school junior, he had started considering colleges. His list included the University of Evansville, Indiana University, Purdue University, and ISU's regional campus. He ultimately decided Indiana State's main campus in Terre Haute – like IU in Bloomington and Purdue in West Lafayette – was simply too far. He preferred to stay close to home. And his grade point average wasn't the best, so he figured he had a better chance to get accepted at the regional campus. Formal acceptance was greeted with relief followed immediately by fear of whether he would be smart enough to earn a degree.

CHAPTER

2

"I really like you, Charlie," Sarah said as they sat holding hands in the Pyramid Lounge shortly after lunch in the nearby University Center grill. It was April 1981. "You, too, Sarah," he smiled. In both cases it was more than "like," though neither had uttered the word "love" in the months they'd dated. Charlie had been astonished how sexually aggressive Sarah was, practically ripping his shirt off and groping him the first time they were alone in his rental house room. It was the night of their third date. He had no condoms, not even thinking he'd need any. Fortunately, Sarah didn't get pregnant before he began using them. They dated often that school year, going to campus events and an occasional movie in the city. Several dates were simply to fast-food restaurants. Neither had much money. Sarah lived in a small house with two girlfriends, both from the Holland/Huntingburg area.

Charlie was six-feet tall, an inch more than his father, and a half-foot above Sarah. Despite not being an athlete and not working out, Charlie was relatively lean. The first time Sarah saw him without a shirt, his well-toned biceps and torso impressed her. In contrast to his thick, black hair that was always perfectly groomed, Sarah kept hers cut short and hated the curl that appeared on humid Ohio River valley days. She was freckled and shapely – a turn-on for Charlie every time he saw her naked – and credited her physique to eating right and jogging or running whenever she had the opportunity. Unlike Charlie, she had a disdain for fast food although occasionally she indulged.

"Hey, gotta get to class," Charlie suddenly realized. Rising quickly, he said, "I'll see you Saturday night, after I get off work."

"I'll meet you there," she replied. Their lips touched quickly and off he went.

Charlie enjoyed being with Sarah and acknowledged she was smarter than he was. She had a dry wit that caused him to sometimes question whether it was sarcasm or humor. She made him feel comfortable and wasn't pretentious, wanting to please rather than be catered to. Sarah often took a negative view of things and that was about the only thing that bothered him about her. He didn't know what it was in her, perhaps something deep-seeded, but he never brought it up, not wanting to take the chance of spoiling the relationship. Having been raised by parents who were always positive thinkers, Charlie didn't like negative people, and he bit his tongue more than once when he and Sarah were together.

★★★★★

Sarah's summer job was as a cashier at a pharmacy in Huntingburg, about eight miles from her home, while Charlie obtained one at Williams Hardware on Jefferson's Main Street. The low wage and cost of operating a car made it impractical to drive to Bob's Burgers, but he was promised a part-time position again once classes resumed in late August.

"Get your ass off that chair and help unload the delivery truck," demanded Eddie Williams. Charlie might have thought Dick Saunders expected a lot from him, but Bob's manager was a pussycat compared to the owner of the hardware store. Williams had a lot at stake financially and was not about to let anyone give less than 100% effort. To him, that would be tantamount to stealing, although he really liked Charlie and saw potential in the young man.

Williams had spent his life savings — $73,500 — to purchase the store in 1970. It sat in the heart of the main thoroughfare, flanked by Millie's Coffee Shoppe and Edith's Florals. The store was one of the oldest buildings in Jefferson, constructed by Jacob Meade in 1890, then changed from Meade's Hardware to Healy's Hardware in 1930 when Thomas Healy purchased it two years after old man Meade died and family members didn't want to continue operating it. Eddie Williams changed the name again when he bought it.

The building was two-story but only the ground floor was used for retail space, additional supplies and a separate, small office. Other inventory was stored on the upper floor, which had a pull-rope cage elevator in the back. The wood floor on the main level was the original one and the three-inch-wide strips showed pedestrian wear and decades of a mixture of grime and polish buildup. When he took over, Eddie's plan was to completely strip the floor and return its original wood tone – likely a medium oak – but he'd never found, or taken, the time in more than ten years.

Typical of buildings constructed in the late nineteenth century, Eddie's store featured fourteen-foot-high ceilings. Round dark metal plates covered twelve-inch holes in the walls toward the back of the store, where metal exhaust pipes from coal-burning stoves had once been. In its early years, the store's heat came from those cast iron stoves. Customers sat around them, discussing their views, all the while depositing chewing tobacco juice into spittoons sitting on the floor at each end of worn wooden benches, likely old church pews. Beginning in the late 1940s, Saturday mornings were especially popular as the problems of the world and the actions or inactions of the U.S. Congress were solved, the poor decisions of the high school basketball coach in the previous night's game analyzed, and prices of hogs, cattle, and grain praised or bemoaned. Everyone had an opinion about everything and if you didn't ask for it, they would tell you anyway. When the stoves were replaced with central heat, the gatherings stopped – the end of an era in Jefferson.

Eddie Williams' store carried virtually every type of hardware item a farmer or town resident would want, some rarely sought. Want milk strainers? Got them.

Tractor axle grease? Got it. Garden seed? Got it. Yes, raccoon traps, automotive engine v-belts, fishing gear, and live bait – minnows and earthworms, too. Eddie was especially proud of the glass case of hunting and camping knives on display because he thought it was the largest variety in the area. He sold Indiana hunting and fishing licenses. And he offered RCA televisions and Whirlpool refrigerators, washers, and dryers. There were few pre-packaged goods like what was sold in more modern stores nearby, especially larger cities such as the county seat of Pemberton or Evansville. Williams' shelves held row after row of bulk screws, bolts, nuts, nails, you name it. There were thousands of items. What made the store popular was the variety, the atmosphere, and the down-to-earth nature of Williams and his employees, no matter how crusty he sometimes seemed.

The steel-gray shelves stood eight feet high, separated by four-foot-wide aisles. Eddie hadn't replaced the shelves when he purchased the property, and their dull appearance came from the passage of time. But they were dust-free, something he insisted on. If an employee had nothing to do, he'd better have a dust cloth or feather duster in hand, or not get caught on their derriere – not the word he used. Various sizes and strengths of rope and metal chains hung on spools along one wall. A large room off the showroom held equipment for cutting pipe, screen wire, and glass. An assortment of clay tile and concrete blocks sat stacked to one side. In a back room were bags of asphalt patch and concrete mix.

Charlie liked Eddie and felt his education at the store that summer was worth as much as the formal one he was paying for at ISUE. Lessons learned working would stay with him throughout life, some of them reflecting the teachings of one or both of his parents – work hard, don't goof off, be respectful, show kindness, understand the customer's needs, empathize with the customer when there is a complaint, do your best to resolve all problems in favor of the customer.

"Look, it's tough to make a good living as an owner," Eddie lamented to Charlie during a teaching moment. "Government regulations and taxes really make it difficult, but there's one thing no one can do better than us and that's how we treat customers. As strange as this may sound to you, we might not have total control of our prices because of competition but we do have *total*" – he emphasized the word – "control of how we treat our customers. It's like a statement I read from someone who was living under the Castro regime in Cuba, *'They can control my body but they can't control my mind.'* If we make customers our friends, they will return again and again, and that's what keeps me in business here in this old store."

CHAPTER
3

For Charlie and Sarah, the 1981-82 school year flew by. That summer, she was back at the pharmacy and he at the hardware store.

"You don't talk that way to any of my employees or to me, for that matter, you understand?" Eddie was overheard nearly shouting into the phone in his office. "We're not sub-humans. We're people who work hard to make a living and treat our customers right." Not pausing for a response, he continued, "If you want to talk to a dog that way, go ahead, but if you want to talk to me or anyone else here, talk to us with some respect, despite whatever the problem is you have. Understand?" Peeking, Charlie could see the veins sticking out in Eddie's neck.

"And you will not cuss when talking to me," Eddie stated sternly into the receiver. "One more cuss word and the receiver will fall from my hand onto the base, we'll be disconnected, and no one – I mean no one – will *ever* be able to help you. Do I make myself clear?" Eddie paused to listen. "All right then, tell me the problem with the refrigerator."

Charlie stood near the open office door but out of sight as Eddie took down details of the customer's complaint. "Hey, Melvin," Eddie stated calmly, "we've known each other a long time. You've been a good customer and I hope you think we've been a good store for you to do business with. I don't blame you for getting upset about the refrigerator not working properly after it's been serviced twice for the same problem." He paused.

"Yes, I know Melvin. It ought to last years without a problem, but sometimes malfunctions happen." He paused again. "Just a moment. Dick handed me your paperwork. Melvin, what I've got here shows you were offered an extended service contract when you bought the refrigerator and you refused. So, now the frig is out of parts and labor warranty and you want me to absorb the expenses. Tell you what I'll do. I'm going to be more than fair with you. If you'll allow the tech to service it again and you pay for parts and labor, if the same malfunction occurs within six months, I'll replace it at no charge to you. Fair enough?" Eddie listened again.

"Good, I'll have Jerry Tevault call and set up an appointment."

The customer said something, then Eddie replied, "That's all right, Melvin. I understand how you can get worked up and say things you don't mean. I accept your apology and I'll pass that on to Dick, too. He's the one you talked with just before me. Have a good day, Melvin."

Just as Charlie passed the door opening, pretending he had come from the back of the store and was oblivious to the phone conversation, Eddie commanded, "Charlie, come here." Charlie wheeled and entered. "I've no doubt that you heard me. My voice got pretty loud. Probably could've been heard at Millie's next door. But that's how to work with customers, especially foul-mouthed belligerent ones. You defuse them, then you work with them. Not all, not by any means, are as difficult as Melvin. I'll stand up for my employees any day and I won't let a customer berate them, or me, the way Melvin talked with Dick on the phone. Luckily, Melvin's the exception. Most customers are reasonable people, even when they have problems with things they buy here."

Charlie nodded.

"Now that's another lesson as a summer employee," Williams smiled.

★★★★★

Jerry Tevault had been Charlie's best friend since elementary school. Jerry didn't follow his classmate to college, electing instead to attend a two-year technical school where he learned the ins and outs of appliances and got a job installing and servicing Eddie Williams' customers' refrigerators, washers, and dryers. He did similar work for an appliance store in Pemberton.

They talked often on the job.

"I think Sarah's a nymphomaniac," Charlie said, not in jest, as they loaded a laundry pair into the bed of Jerry's beat-up eight-year-old black Chevy pickup in June. "God, she's killing me."

"Nice problem to have," Jerry replied, his smirking face clearly visible. "Why can't I have luck like that?"

"No, I'm serious," Charlie replied as he grunted while they lifted the dryer into the bed. "There's almost never a day or night when I see her that we don't have sex. I'm beginning to wonder if she's interested in me for the sex and not for who I am as a person."

"You're complaining?" Jerry frowned.

"Not complaining. Just wondering, that's all."

"Well, it's not the kind of thing most guys worry about. Count your blessings. Maybe this is just a summertime thing and it'll wear off when school starts."

"I'm not so certain," Charlie replied. "We were pretty active last school year." The two loaded the washer and used rope to secure both appliances so they wouldn't slide or get picked up by air draft when Jerry drove down the highway.

Slamming the tailgate shut, Charlie confided, "The other thing that bothers me is how negative Sarah can be. She's a sweet girl, really sweet, and we like each other a lot, but, man, does she complain, almost always seeing things from a negative viewpoint. Like the 'glass half empty' expression. I see possibilities in everything. Not Sarah."

"Have you talked to her about it?" Jerry inquired.

"Not directly. I've skirted the issue but it's building in me."

"Man, I'm not an expert since I don't date that much," Jerry replied. "But if it's really bothering you, I'd tackle it right away. Might as well do it now and see what happens. Better sooner than later."

"Yeah, you're probably right," Charlie said.

Charlie and Sarah got together every Sunday afternoon, usually at her parents' farm house about forty minutes east of Jefferson. The farm was two miles from Holland, and Jordan Carter made his living from oats, wheat, corn, and milk, the latter from a small herd of Holstein. His education from the time he was born in the same house where Sarah grew up was the land, not school. The 230 acres were treeless and rolling, with two ponds – stocked with bluegill and small-mouth bass in one and catfish in the other – that provided occasional recreation and a family meal. Mildred Carter, Sarah's mother, was a homemaker and, like her husband, not educated beyond high school. Each was short and both carried more weight than they wanted. Sarah was their only child.

An unpainted barn with stalls for cattle and loose and baled hay and straw in the loft stood on a lot beside a one-story, white, cinder block milking building. Jordan Carter's John Deere tractor, combine, and other field equipment were in an adjacent metal-framed structure. The two-story, white, wood-framed house was about 200 feet away. A wide slat swing hung from once-bright silver chains on the porch that faced the gravel road in front of the house. Jordan and Mildred tried to spend at least a couple of hours on the porch after he finished milking the cows late Sunday afternoons, when the weather was nice.

Sitting in the swing on a sunny but not terribly hot July afternoon, Sarah complained, "My job is so boring, so dull. I get so darned tired of hearing about every ache and pain of all those *old* people who come in. *'Arthur Itis is raising his ugly head again today. I can hardly move.'*" She changed her voice tone and inflection with each statement. "*'Rain must be comin', my knees are really achin' today.'*" Another. "*'Just cain't get rid of this here cold.'*"

"I don't get paid enough to listen to all those complaints, day after day after day. I'm really not that interested in how those people feel!"

Charlie bristled. Turning to face her, he scolded, "Shame on you, Sarah. Your pharmacy exists for one reason and that's to serve those 'old' people, as you put it, and help them get well. No sick people, no pharmacy, no job. Pretty simple!"

He could feel his face reddening, his tone stern. "I'm disappointed in you. Number one, you're lucky to have a summer job. We both know lots of friends who can't even find one with this recession we're in. Number two, as I recall, you gladly accepted the job offer and the wage because you were fortunate to find something. Number three, I'm tired of hearing you complain about everything."

The next words were those he later wished he'd not uttered, and as he was about to say them he thought he shouldn't. But his seldom-used temper prevailed.

"Yes, I'm sick and tired of you complaining. I've never talked to you about it, but as long as I've known you, you've had negative comments about almost everything in your life." Charlie kept up the barrage. "Life isn't that bad, Sarah. Life is good. Life is filled with positives, like your mental and physical health, your ability to attend college, your loving parents, me, freedoms."

As he talked, Charlie didn't like what he was seeing in Sarah's face. He thought he'd touch some feelings of remorse. Instead, all he saw was an icy, cold stare. *Should I stop?* No.

"You have great parents. I see in them love, compassion, understanding. I never hear negative comments from them. Why you are different, I don't understand. I want you to see the positive side of life because that's the type of person I want to be with, maybe spend my life with."

Charlie had never broached the subject of marriage and he surprised himself, but it was a natural part of what he was attempting to convey to this woman he loved.

Sarah just sat there, not moving a muscle, staring at him – staring a hole through him. There were no moistening eyes, no tears, no admission, no promise to change.

Suddenly, she rose from the swing. "Well, if that's the way you feel, Charlie, then I'll ask you to leave right now." Swinging her right arm and pointing toward his car in the gravel driveway between the house and the barn lot, "Get off this porch. Now! Go!"

"Sarah, don't act that way," Charlie pleaded. "I just want to help you turn your attitude around. Don't turn against *me*, for God's sake!"

Continuing to point toward the car, she ordered "Go, Charlie. Go home. If you think I'm that bad, we shouldn't see each other. I'm sorry I've disappointed you. I thought we were in love. People in love don't say such cruel things to one another."

Charlie stood his ground. "Yes, they do, Sarah. Love means people want to help each other, they care deeply for one another and want them to be special in this world."

Her hands now on her hips, "Love doesn't mean you say such hateful words, Charlie. You've been mean and I don't deserve it. You don't deserve me. Now get off this porch. I mean it!" Her face was ashen and her hazel eyes were piercing, like a menacing cat.

"Sarah."

"Charlie. Go home!" She slammed the front door behind her as she entered the house.

His shoulders drooped. His head slumped as he walked to his car. He was devastated, consumed by a feeling of remorse – not at what he'd said but how Sarah had taken it. His words were a knife in her side. Painful. Unexpected.

He didn't sleep.

At work the next morning, Eddie approached. "Charlie, I need you to take the pickup to Corydon. The asphalt and concrete company I use has my order for two dozen bags of patch and mix. The weather looks good so you shouldn't need a tarp to cover them."

Charlie checked the fuel gauge to ensure he had enough for the 160-mile round trip, then headed south toward I-64. He'd been listless that morning from the time he got out of bed and ate a bowl of cereal without speaking to his mom or dad until Eddie asked him to make the trip.

As he drove east on the interstate, his emotions caved in. His soft crying was followed by sobbing, and his chest heaved as he called out, "Why'd she take it that way? My God, I've lost her. Saraahhh," he shouted. A woman in the passing car was staring at him.

His vision so blurred he could hardly see the pavement, Charlie exited at the first rest area. Following the "cars" sign, he drove to the farthest end and pulled into the last parking space and walked up the hill that overlooked a valley where it seemed the distant hills were ten miles away. Walking in grass, his head down, no one anywhere near him, he began talking in short sentences, in staccato, to space that had no ears and made no response.

"What have I done?" he cried out. "What have I done? I've destroyed her. I'll never see her again. Why'd she get so upset? How else could I have said it? Sarah, please don't take this out on me. You've got to understand." Charlie was meandering with no clear direction. He was numb. His head drooped and he stood and stared, but he focused on nothing.

Suddenly, snapping to reality, Charlie looked at his watch and realized he was thirty minutes behind in the trip to Corydon.

"What the hell's wrong with you?" Eddie inquired when Charlie returned to the store. "Your eyes are red as hell and sunken like a sink hole. You OK? Sick? Need to go home?"

"Naw, I'm all right," Charlie pretended. "Think dust in the air at the plant irritated the eyes. Should clear up soon." Eddie accepted the explanation and walked away.

Charlie knew where to unload the heavy bags, which he did without thinking. Life had left his body.

★★★★★

A day went by. Then another. Then two more. Then a week. No call from Sarah.

Finally, on Tuesday, he called Fenneman's Pharmacy in Huntingburg. "Could I speak with Sarah Carter, please?"

"Just a moment. I'll go get her."

Charlie waited.

The voice returned. "Who's calling, please?"

"Please tell her it's Charlie."

A pause. "Uh, Sarah's not here right now. Uh, she took a late lunch. May I take a message?"

Charlie knew the person was lying.

"Just tell her Charlie called."

Another day. Then another. On Friday evening, Charlie called Sarah's house.

"Mrs. Carter, it's Charlie Simpson. Is Sarah home?"

"Well, hello, Charlie. I missed seeing you Sunday? You okay?"

"Yes, ma'am, just fine."

"You coming over this Sunday?

"I'm not sure. Guess that will be up to Sarah."

"Why's that, Charlie? Is something wrong? Come to think of it, Sarah hasn't been herself lately."

"Well, I'd love to talk with her."

"She's with her girlfriends, tonight, Charlie. Can I have her call you?"

"Yes, ma'am. And thanks."

He remained heartbroken and listless, and tried not to show it at home or at the store but suspected family and friends knew something was wrong.

The weekend went by, then three more days. On Thursday night, just before 10, the phone rang. Charlie was watching television in his room at his parents' house. His dad answered and knocked on the bedroom door. "Phone for you, Charlie. Not certain who it is, but they're pretty upset." Charlie heard sobbing as he answered.

"Oh, Charlie, forgive me," the voice cried. "Forgive me for what I've been, who I've been. Forgive me for being the most horrible person in the world." Then the words he would remember forever. "I love you, Charlie. I want to spend my life with you. I promise to change. I promise you will find a new me, but I need your help at every step." More sobbing. "It won't be easy for me but I'll change. Please forgive me, please," Sarah pleaded in words that were hardly recognizable through her throaty crying.

"Forgive *you*?" Charlie responded. "I should ask you to forgive *me*," he said in a most compassionate way. "I should never have talked to you like I did."

"Yes, you should have," Sarah sobbed. "I deserved it, everything you said. I've talked with my minister and I spent Friday night with friends who admitted they'd wanted to tell me to stop being so negative. My minister asked me to pray for help in making changes and my friends said I should hug you with all my breath for having the nerve to confront me." More sobs. "Oh, Charlie, I need you. I need to be with you."

"Dad, I'm going to Sarah's," Charlie said to his father as he walked through the living room where Horace was watching television.

"What? At this late hour? Why Charlie, it's after ten."

"Yeah, I know, Dad, but she and I need to talk things out."

"Is something wrong?"

"Just the opposite, Dad. Just the opposite."

Horace watched Charlie walk out the door. *Sometimes,* he thought, *I just don't understand that boy.*

Sarah burst from the house the moment Charlie's car pulled into the driveway and he shut off the engine.

She ravished him in the front seat. Forgiveness, longing, all wrapped up in a flurry of emotion with the man she hoped to marry.

"Come with me," she commanded, as she opened the passenger door.

Sarah took Charlie by the hand and they walked – she was pulling hard – to the barn. Without a word, Sarah stepped onto the bottom rung of the built-in wall ladder that led to the loft. Naked bulbs that hung above the cattle stalls cast dim light above.

"Come here, lover," she commanded with a guttural tone he'd not heard before. "I've always wanted you here." Charlie'd discovered in the car she wore no bra or panties. He was turned on.

Their embrace was sudden and almost animalistic, and they fell to the thick, soft bed of loose straw on the loft floor. In an instant, he'd pushed her blouse above her naked breasts, two buttons bouncing away in the process, and she'd unbuckled his belt. As she pulled up her skirt, he pushed his jeans to his ankles and was almost immediately inside her.

Their heavy breathing and moaning masked movement on the straw behind Charlie. All he could recall later was excruciating pain from the blow to his head.

Sarah screamed but there was no one to hear her, no one to save her. Her parents' bedroom was on the other side of the house and they always slept with a window air conditioner running in the summer. She tried kicking, tried getting up from the straw, but the older man with breath so foul she thought she'd vomit was on her just as Charlie had been, but pinning her wrists so tightly she believed the bones surely would break.

"Don't think yer gonna get help, little darlin'," he grunted as he tried to penetrate her. "There ain't no one gonna come runnin'." Sarah started to scream again, but the attacker let go of her left wrist and slapped her face so hard with his right hand she felt the warmth of blood in a corner of her mouth. But she continued to struggle, resisting his attempt to get inside her.

In an instant, he let go of the same wrist long enough to produce a large hunting knife with a razor thin cutting edge that he now held at her neck. "You want me to cut that pretty little face of yours?" he threatened.

With that, Sarah froze. Any potential sound was caught in her throat. Her eyes, equally frozen with fear, were transfixed on his face. In the dim light she could see his uneven teeth and unshaven face.

"Now that's better," he grunted. "Just open up or this blade might slide through that pumped up big vein in your neck and produce a pretty, dark red Old Faithful."

Sarah later recalled to detectives that she saw a blur at that moment – the blur from the same piece of 2x4 wood, now wielded by Charlie – swung with such force that Sarah's attacker was knocked to the floor. Charlie swung again and hit the top of the man's head. As he did, Charlie's feet slipped on the straw under him and he fell onto his back. He shook his head, attempting to clear his senses. The attacker struggled to his feet, knife in hand and moved toward Charlie. As he did, Charlie pulled back his legs and kicked with every ounce of strength in him. The assailant fell – almost flew – backwards and over the edge of the loft. Charlie and Sarah grimaced when they heard what sounded like bone snapping as the body hit the hard dirt floor below. Charlie rose, looked down at the lifeless form, then grabbed Sarah in a bear hug.

Police identified the man as Elmer Clifton, a sixty-year-old drifter wanted as a suspect in a series of farm house break-ins in the Jefferson area. Not only had Clifton died of a broken neck, the knife he'd held was found buried in his chest.

Sarah was taken by ambulance to the hospital emergency room in Jasper. Doctors confirmed she had not been sexually penetrated but there was bruising on her inner thighs, upper arms, and neck, a cut of a corner of her mouth, and severe contusions to her wrists. "You're a lucky woman," the examining physician told her. "There's an inch-long, very thin mark on your neck – not enough to draw blood – but apparently caused by something sharp." Stunned by the trauma of what had happened, Sarah still remembered the knife. Her body shook. She was given Valium to keep her calm.

The Dubois County Sheriff's Department interviewed both Sarah and Charlie, who had ridden with her in the ambulance. Charlie held up well emotionally and was able to explain all he could about the incident, despite the fact he'd been struck hard by the 2x4. An egg-sized bump had formed on the side of his head by the time they reached the hospital and there were cuts around it but none required stitches. He had a severe headache and was in an adjoining exam room while doctors kept watch for any signs of a concussion. There was none.

Based on his department's findings from interviews with the couple and on the coroner's initial report, the sheriff quickly cleared Charlie and Sarah of any wrongdoing.

Both sought counseling and Sarah's emotional scars were deep. Her body had not been penetrated by Clifton but her mind had.

She saw a female clinical social worker who specialized in sexual trauma cases. Sarah's mother drove her to appointments in Evansville three times the first week and then twice each week for another month. Eventually, the sessions were only weekly and throughout her junior year. Her grades suffered, and she needed Charlie's emotional and physical strength. As often as possible, he went with her. He was seeing a male psychotherapist in the same office.

Initially, Sarah and her clinical social worker, Nicole Bartley, talked and worked through what happened the night of the attack and the overpowering feeling that had captivated Sarah's thoughts – day and night – of what happened – the horror of seeing Charlie struck, the revolting man on top of her, trying to rape her while threatening with the knife, then Charlie and the assailant struggling, and, finally, the sickening sound of the neck breaking when the body slammed into the floor below. She shuddered every time she thought of it, often when alone in the dark of her room at night, unable to sleep.

"Sarah, there's a relatively new term for what has happened to you," said the specialist. "It's called Posttraumatic Stress Disorder. It's nothing for you to fear, but based on what you've been experiencing, the symptoms fit with PTSD. That means I – we – have a better understanding of how to help you deal with this and eventually get it behind you." She paused, "Look at me." Sarah saw the compassion in Nicole Bartley's eyes and the smile on her face. Both said "comfort." "Trust." "Hope." "You *will* overcome this and become the woman you were before."

There were joint counseling sessions with Charlie when the social worker led Sarah from the past to thinking about the future, to helping her begin to feel whole again, to feel comfortable with her body and to discuss her needs with Charlie. Sarah knew it would take time to become comfortable with Charlie again. He had become a pillar of strength to her and never suffered long-term effects from the incident. His clinical social worker was amazed at his resilience.

In additional to her individual therapy meetings with Bartley, Sarah participated in group sessions, with other women who had experienced rape or sexual assault. Each was in her own stage of recovery, and their stories of how they were dealing with their moment of trauma – the majority, but not all, successfully – gave Sarah encouragement and eventually courage to take control of her path to emotional freedom.

Charlie, in his final year at the university, was with Sarah as often as possible. They talked, held one another, hugged. "Charlie, you are so patient, so understanding, so comforting," she would say. "I could not climb this mountain without you."

By the end of the school year, Sarah appeared to be much like she was before the previous summer's incident. She and Charlie felt very much in love. There was no sex. He would wait for her initiation.

Elmer Clifton left behind two sons who had lived with him at a ramshackle trailer in northern Kentucky, about sixty miles south of Holland. They knew the area where their dad died because they'd hunted wild game in the fields and fished in lakes there. "That damned guy ruined everything," Austin Clifton said to his brother. "Yeah, we'll show him a thing or two one of these days," Jeremiah vowed.

CHAPTER

4

"Charles, do you take Sarah to be your wedded wife......"

The ceremony at the Carters' church, St. Paul Lutheran, couldn't have been more perfect, Sarah reflected yet again, days later, as she and Charlie lay on the beach at Hilton Head Island, South Carolina. It was a warm, but not humid, October morning in 1985. Although Sarah didn't show sexual passion as she had prior to the attempted rape in the summer three years earlier, their honeymoon had plenty of it from the moment they checked into their hotel, only taking occasional breaks for food and sunning or walking hand-in-hand along the shore. They talked lovingly of starting a family one day, agreeing that two or three children would be ideal. A week at Hilton Head was just the respite both needed before returning to their jobs.

Sarah loved teaching fine art at Tecumseh High School in a nearby county and Charlie felt challenged in his management role at Eddie Williams' hardware store. He'd considered employment elsewhere with his business management degree, but Eddie's offer of a buy-in to ownership and the possibility of owning the store outright someday were too enticing. Eddie respected Charlie's work ethic, intelligence, and customer skills and with neither of his children having any interest in the business, he saw in Charlie an opportunity for the future. Charlie had something he didn't – a college degree. Charlie knew from Eddie how challenging it was to make a profit but he also knew there were no other major competitors in the area. Perhaps using what he'd learned about management in his studies he might be able to persuade Eddie to make some needed upgrades while still maintaining the old-fashioned traditions.

★★★★★

The morning of September 13, 2001 – two days after the attacks on the World Trade Center towers in New York City and the Pentagon in Washington, D.C. – Charlie received a telephone call that would change his life.

"Charlie, it's Liz." He knew the voice, of course – Eddie's wife, Elizabeth; "Liz" to almost everyone. Charlie was amazed at the strength of her voice when she uttered, "Charlie, Eddie's dead." He was stunned.

"I'd set the alarm for 5 like I always do, because Eddie likes to get up early before going to the store. I shook him and said, 'Another work day, Eddie,' as I rolled out of bed. I went to the kitchen to pour a cup of coffee that had brewed when the timer went off at 4:45. I always set a cup on the bathroom sink counter so Eddie will have it when he gets up. As I walked through the bedroom, I said, 'Hey, sleepy-head, time to get up.' I sat the cup in the bathroom and came back to the bed and shook Eddie again. He didn't move. I started screaming."

Charlie didn't interrupt. He sensed Liz needed to talk.

"The funeral home took Eddie, and our doctor came to our house and gave me a sedative. You're my third call, behind my kids. Oh, Charlie, I don't know what I'm going to do."

"Oh, God, Liz, I'm so, so sorry. I'm just staggered by this." He thought how useless that comment was. "Of course, you know that. Don't worry about the store, Liz. I'll handle everything. The guys and I will keep everything going without fail."

"Thanks, Charlie. You're like a son to me, and you are – were – to Eddie. Just keep it going and we'll talk later."

★★★★★

Liz sold the store to Charlie six months later. Her two children – one a dentist in California and the other a lawyer in Kentucky – wanted nothing to do with it. Eddie was sixty-six and Liz a year younger but she preferred the money over the financial risk, long hours, and all the other challenges of running a business.

Charlie was forty. He and Sarah had been somewhat frugal in their spending over the years. Their home was a modest brick ranch. It was their second house in the sixteen years they'd been married and they felt comfortable in it. He'd been making payments from his biweekly paycheck toward paying off his piece of store ownership, so the amount Liz wanted for the remaining stock – the majority – was within reach, using savings and a loan from Jefferson National Bank. Eddie had begrudgingly changed some of the ways the business operated but now Charlie would have no one to stand in the way of others he had longed to make.

He and Sarah had no children. He blamed himself. Her gynecologist assured them that the attempted rape had no bearing, had not caused Sarah anxiety severe enough to affect her ability to get pregnant. Over the years since they married, Sarah had occasional nightmares and would awaken with her nightgown soaking wet. Rarely did she seek counseling but she found in Charlie the solace she needed. Sarah fell deeper in love.

They'd endured countless tests and attempts at a pregnancy, but to no avail. Both accepted their circumstances and neither wanted to adopt, but they vowed to be of help to youth and youth groups as best they could. Charlie did that through business ads in high school athletic and musical event printed programs and Sarah through her work at school.

★★★★★

As Charlie learned in his college studies two decades earlier, it was one thing to be the assistant coach, the deputy director or the vice president, but when all responsibilities fell on one person's shoulders, the challenges grew exponentially. The biggest was the financial side.

The loan from Jefferson National included funds that allowed him to make immediate changes in the store's layout. He had the pitted hardwood floor covered with a medium gray tile. The decades-old shelves were replaced with shorter, white metal ones and the array of products was reduced so that the shelves held fewer items, and the aisles were made wider. Walls were painted a lighter gray than the floor tile. For better inventory control, and somewhat to his chagrin because it meant giving up the "we have anything and everything" feel, Charlie brought in more prepackaged goods, such as nuts, bolts, and washers, to replace the loose volume of those items in large bins. Customer theft had always been a problem with them anyway. A cash register system with a bar code reader was purchased. More ceiling lighting was added. Charlie reveled in customer comments that the store was more attractive and felt larger.

Complaints were inevitable. "Charlie, why the hell do I have to buy all these nuts when I only need two?" Ned Fowler questioned, handing over a plastic bag containing an assortment of twelve nuts, and not in a friendly way.

"Ned, I know it's a pain in the butt, but I just can't afford to sell so many items in the bulk anymore. All I can ask is that you appreciate the fact I'm here for you, and I'll do my best to have whatever you need in hardware even if sometimes, like these nuts, you need to take home more than you'd like at the moment. I'm guessing that over time you'll need more and you'll already have them."

Charlie watched Ned shrug his shoulders and walk out after he'd made the purchase. Charlie wondered if he'd be back.

★★★★★

Over the next decade and a half, Simpson Hardware had good times and tough ones. Personally, it was a difficult period for Charlie and Sarah. Three of their parents died between 2003 and 2011. Charlie's mother passed away much earlier, in 1991. His father seemed to have no problem living alone, then he died from a massive stroke at home twelve years later. Charlie had stayed in close touch with Horace who lived about three-quarters of a mile from him. Sunday noon meals were typically spent with Horace one Sunday and the Carters the other as long as Charlie and Sarah had been married.

Simpson Hardware's business flourished for a five-year period beginning in 2002. The refreshing look of the store's interior, an unwavering commitment to a mantra *'If we excel at serving the customer, profits will naturally follow,'* and the addition of one full-time and two part-time positions – taking the total staff to eight – resulted in booming times. But the Great Recession began in 2007 and for the next few years, the business struggled. In 2009, Charlie had to eliminate the three positions he'd created. He also stopped selling large appliances and electronics that had been a store staple dating back to Eddie's days. "I carry 'want' and 'need' products," he told Sarah. "People want televisions, but not when times are bad. They need washers, dryers, and refrigerators but if I'm getting out of electronics, I might as well get out of the other stuff, too. I'll have less money tied up in inventory." Small kitchen appliances such as toaster ovens, mixers, and electric can openers would continue to be part of his inventory.

Besides the recession, another blow was the opening of a mega HardwareMart store only ten miles from Jefferson. It was more than ten times the size of

Simpson Hardware. HardwareMart was a national chain operating in thirty states and, as with Walmart expansions, its size of offerings and low prices pressured smaller retailers.

"I can't imagine them opening during this damned recession," Charlie lamented to Sarah and his employees. "But I'll give 'em credit for the move. If they can establish a good reputation during tough times, they'll be a monster to deal with once the economy improves." Although Charlie advertised little – primarily fliers inserted in the county newspaper – he decided not to attempt any major sales event when HardwareMart had its two-week grand opening. "No sense being embarrassed with any pricing I'd have in our ads and I can't afford to take prices ridiculously low just to compete in the paper anyway. But," he told the staff, "never lose a deal if you can help it. Come to me if you're not certain what to do when someone says HardwareMart or anyone else has a lower price. And, for God's sake, show the greatest friendliness and care for the customer you possibly can. Nobody can 'out nice' us. Plus, they can't out clean us. Every inch of this store must be kept as spotless as possible every hour we're open."

Sarah had wanted to retire in 2009 after twenty-five years of teaching but Charlie pleaded with her to continue.

"Thank God for your salary over the years, sweetheart. If we hadn't salted away as much as we did, I don't know where we'd be today. But we're going to take a big hit from the new competition, at least for a while, then we'll have to see how things shake out." He asked for five more years. "How about 2014 as a retirement date? By then, I hope the store will be in good shape again and Congress will have given us small business owners some tax breaks."

CHAPTER 5

Looking up from the record books and sheets of paper on the kitchen table, Charlie sighed, "Sarah, we're just not making it." It was April 2016. "As hard as I'm trying, the store's just not turning enough profit to meet all the bills and the damned taxes. Ineffective Congress! Taxes are killing us. So is freaking HardwareMart. You know, I really thought that after the initial sales dip when they opened, we'd be okay. But loyalty anymore is who has the best price. It's so damned tough to compete with a national chain."

Sarah stepped from the sink behind him and placed her hands on Charlie's shoulders. He turned in the chair and the deep lines in his forehead showed the worry. He saw her tears.

Rising and taking her hands in his, "Dear, it's not that we're not making a living, we're just not eking out enough to put back into the business so we can make improvements to the store, make it look even more appealing, more up-to-date, more inviting. For goodness sake, don't worry."

"I shouldn't have retired," she lamented.

He took her in his arms. "Don't say that, Sarah. You worked *thirty* years, five more than you wanted. I could never have asked for more than what you did for the two of us. At the same time, I know it was a job you loved. Teaching was your life, your inspiration. Seeing children grow at school was huge satisfaction for you."

She pulled her arms free and raised both hands to the sides of his face, then slowly, lightly, massaged his temples with her fingertips. "Charlie, I'm worried about you," she said softly. "You need to take a break, get away from work for several days, maybe a week. It would do you good." He said nothing. "I'm dead serious. You should see your eyes. You're *so* tired."

"But how the hell you expect me to get away, Sarah? Who's gonna' oversee everything if I'm gone? Damn, it's just not that easy."

She didn't back down. "Dick can do it. He's been with you ten years and you've even said he was someone you could trust with the last dime you had. You just need to give him a chance to show he can manage the store while you're gone." Sarah shifted her eyes to his chest while gathering thoughts, then looked at him again. "Your problem is you think you're the sole answer to every problem and you have to micro manage without giving others leeway to show what they can do. Let me tell you something, the store can definitely get along without you. You've got a great staff and they won't let you down. In fact, they'd love the opportunity to show you how effective they'd be."

Charlie said nothing. He stared down at Sarah. Pushing back, he said, "Okay, maybe you're right. Maybe I should catch a break for myself. I'm sure not getting one from the government." Knowing her persuasion had won out, Sarah stifled a grin. Surrendering, Charlie said, "I'll talk with Dick and see if he'd be comfortable with me being gone for a few days."

"Not a few days, Charlie, at least a week. We can go camping, drive to Nashville to the Grand Ole Opry, or anything else, just to get away. It'll do you good."

★★★★★

The three-hour drive to St. Louis on I-64 was as refreshing as just getting away from Jefferson and work. Charlie elected to take the Chevrolet Malibu instead of his pickup truck since the sedan would get much better gas mileage. Neither said a word as they listened to Prime Country on XM radio and occasionally glanced at one another and smiled. It would be good to see the Cardinals play again. It'd been three years since Charlie attended a major league baseball game, the last when the Cards beat the Pirates down the stretch in the pennant race. Jefferson was in the heart of Indiana's Cardinals' fan base, and Charlie had been a staunch follower of the club all his life.

Queen of the Internet when it came to finding deals, Sarah got a hotel room for $83 a night only eight blocks from Busch Stadium. The two early-season games were nighttime affairs, so she and Charlie planned one day at the St. Louis Zoo and another touring the Arch and other sites depending on the amount of time they had. Giving in to Charlie that he only spend four days away from his store was not what Sarah wanted, but at least she got him away from the daily grind. She knew it would do him good.

"This ravioli sauce is superb," Sarah remarked after taking a sip of Cabernet Sauvignon at the Italian restaurant where they dined two blocks from their hotel the evening of their arrival. "Thank you for wanting to come here, Charlie. I really appreciate it. You have no idea how happy I am tonight." She showed him when they got back to the hotel.

★★★★★

"Senator Barbara Lansing said today she has a plan for breaking the gridlock that has prevented Congress from enacting any significant legislation this year," the correspondent reported on the radio newscast Charlie and Sarah heard en route back to Jefferson. *"The California Republican who is believed far ahead in the race for her party's presidential nomination in late July said her plan would include major compromises with the opposition party. Meanwhile, the man expected to be her Democratic opponent, South Carolina congressman Bobby Gilford, was on the campaign trail in*

North Dakota......" Charlie lowered the volume. "Break the gridlock, my ass. Congress is so screwed up no one is going to break that gridlock. We'd be better off if we threw every one of those incompetents out and started all over," he blared. Sarah said nothing, looking straight ahead.

Just as he made the comment, Charlie saw HardwareMart beside the interstate not far from the exit that would take them north to Jefferson, and, suddenly, he forgot all about the fun and relaxation of the days in St. Louis. Reality had returned.

★★★★★

"Business was fairly slow, Charlie," Dick Jones reported when Charlie and Sarah stopped by the store in the late afternoon before going on home. "Customers must have known you were gone," he chuckled. Charlie didn't see much humor in the remark, his mind on the lack of business. "Well, tomorrow will be another day," Charlie sighed as he turned back toward the entrance. Then he stopped, faced his long-time employee, held out his hand, and said, "Thanks, Dick, for watching over everything. I really appreciate it. It was good to get away for a few days. And, by the way, the floors and everything look great."

Charlie was half paying attention as the television news anchor reported another drop in voter confidence in Congress, tying an all-time low since polling began. Sitting in his favorite chair in the living room – the recliner – he perked up enough to hear the newscaster say apathy had swept the nation in numbers never seen before.

That night, he tossed and turned in bed. He decided something had to be done. Could his store continue to survive on the profit margins that had grown thinner since the mega store opened just down I-64? Was Congress ever going to pass any meaningful tax reform legislation that would lower the rate for small businesses like his? He knew he wasn't the only Jefferson business owner who had such concerns.

Out of frustration, he developed a plan.

CHAPTER

6

"Thanks, each of you, for meeting me here," Charlie said to Jason Carlson of Jason's 5 & 10 variety store, Jack Peterson, Peterson's Electronics & Appliances, and Mary Carnahan, as tough-minded a business person as anyone in Jefferson.

Over an hour-and-a-half of much more conversation than food in a back booth at Millie's Coffee Shoppe, Charlie's idea was discussed and a plan of action defined. Each had contacts in other towns and would enlist them to help spread the word.

★★★★★

"You are invited to a discussion of what we small business owners can do about the inactions of our federal legislators," read the handbill under the title

HOPEWELL COUNTY SMALL BUSINESS OWNERS
NON-POLITICAL MEETING
TUESDAY, MAY 17, 7 p.m.
JEFFERSON TOWN HALL

An Act of Frustration

This meeting is organized by local business owners and is intended only for owners of small businesses in Hopewell County or their representatives.

★★★★★

Copies of the flier were distributed by hand in Jefferson, Pemberton, and all other towns in the county. The Hopewell County Business Development Office attached it to a mass email sent to its membership.

"Charlie, can you believe this, this turnout?" Sarah exclaimed, firmly squeezing his right bicep. Rows of gray metal folding chairs began filling thirty minutes before the starting time. "How thrilling," she said. He patted her hand, then broke from her grasp to greet some who had not taken seats.

"Charlie Simpson," he said as he held out his hand. "Omer Hardin, from Devaney," replied a tall, thin, balding man who smiled as he gripped Charlie's fingers like a vice. "So you're the one who organized this, I understand."

"Myself and a few others," Charlie responded.

"Well, Mr. Simpson, I own a grocery and I'm about as fed up as everyone else likely is in this room, so I hope something concrete will come from this meeting. Surely, we can do something Congress can't, and that's make some decisions."

"Omer, if I may call you that, I'll sure appreciate your input tonight…and, by the way, it's Charlie." He smiled, as did Hardin.

The room was a cacophony of noise from nearly one hundred men and women, and two teenaged boys who were already absorbed in their iPhones, before the man behind the microphone at the lectern spoke. "Ladies and gentlemen, kindly take a seat and we'll get this meeting underway." He waited for the sounds to abate.

"My name's Jeff Roberts and I head your county business development office. Most of you, I believe, are members of the organization." Adjusting his tie – one of the few in the room – and looking around at the many faces before him, "Thank you for coming here this evening. I must say that the organizers weren't expecting this large of a turnout. In fact, I'm somewhat blown away. What it says to me is obvious – you are deeply concerned about the state of affairs in Washington and you want to do something or, at least, want something done about it." He saw heads nodding in agreement around the room.

"We in the BDO want more action in Congress, too. Now that doesn't mean we'll be part of whatever you decide tonight – if you should decide anything – but we'll be supportive of local actions that will lead to an improvement of the county business climate."

"That sounds like a cop-out," someone yelled from a back row.

"Now, Sam, it's not. All I'm saying is that whatever comes out of this meeting will not necessarily be part of an action plan by our organization. This meeting was planned by Jefferson business owners and we were pleased to help get the word out. Certainly, we're going to be extremely interested in the outcome.

"Let me turn this podium over to Mary Carnahan, one of the four who organized tonight's meeting."

Roberts nodded to Carnahan, a stocky, graying, woman whose reddish, wrinkled fingers clutching the lectern were that of a person who made her living working on heavy equipment, often out of doors. Carnahan surveyed the crowd, adjusted the microphone downward, then stated, "I don't mind telling my age – I'm 60 – and I've worked hard all my life. My husband died five years ago, leaving me with the truck servicing and wrecker business on the south edge of town." She introduced Charlie, Jason, and Jack.

"The four of us were talking and we're sick and tired of the do-nothing Congress, and that includes our area's congressman. There are many matters that need attention, yet the two political parties can't seem to agree on any of it. Some of it gets hearings that don't result in any action. Some items get to the House or Senate floor and are filibustered to death. No wonder the American people don't trust their senators and representatives, and see nothing but a waste of money going to their salaries. Plus there's a lame duck president who isn't going to do anything. We think that as small business owners we need to lend our voices in some fashion to let Congress know how fed up we are." Applause filled the room.

Carnahan continued. "Now you may wonder why I'm not including state government in my remarks. I guess I'd say that while we might not be real happy with our Indiana legislators and governor, they seem to get a *few* things done. What we'd like to hear from you is what it is you want Congress to act on, whether it directly affects your business or not. What is it that *you* want Congress to do?" she asked, then waited. She held a notebook and pen.

Silence prevailed before someone yelled out, "Tax code reform. Taxes hurt my business significantly." Another spoke up: "Yeah, tax reform. The laws are too confusing." From elsewhere in the room, "Immigration. I need migrant workers but I have to know whether they have to be legal or not." One by one, other voices sounded. Carnahan scribbled as fast as she could. "A crackdown on online retailers who don't charge Indiana sales tax." "Full repeal of the estate tax." "Health care – reach down to the very small companies and allow them to make health care more affordable for their employees."

When it appeared there would be no further suggestions, Carnahan introduced Charlie.

Months of long hours in the store and constant worry over his business's finances had built stress that was ready to spill out of Charlie. He sensed his emotions the moment he stood up and walked to the lectern; an odd feeling as he'd never had many opportunities to talk before audiences and he certainly wasn't at ease behind a microphone. But something seemed different now.

He spoke without notes.

"Those of us in business today – and the majority of our customers – weathered the terrible economic downturn that began in '07-'08 and lasted too many years. We tightened our business operating belts and did whatever we could to stay afloat. Many of our business colleagues didn't make it and many families lost jobs with no way to pay bills. At my store we kept our costs down, treated people fairly, and tried to save a little money. I suppose you did the same." He paused and felt on the verge of tears. "I think of my parents, who were simple and hard-working, not highly educated people. They trusted government officials to look out for them. But those days of trust are gone."

Charlie's pace increased. "Hurting me – and likely many of you – are the big box stores. I recall the song that country music's Alan Jackson sang many years ago, in which he lamented the loss of the little man whose companies went out of the business because of huge discounters that moved into their area. Those same large companies are so big they demand low prices from manufacturers and offer them to consumers. That makes it tough on us, but we have to stay competitive as best we can. I try to support local high school kids with their activities, churches and civic organizations with sponsorships, and I take out ads in community event fliers. The big boxes don't do that, at least in Jefferson." His voice broke with emotion. He pounded the top of the lectern. "All they do is take, take, take and give nothing back to help their towns. So we need tax reform for small businesses like us. With competition as it is, I don't make enough money to plow back into my business and help it grow."

Heavy applause.

Charlie paused and surveyed a room that quickly became so quiet he thought surely everyone could hear his heart thumping.

Then, his voice grew slightly louder. "As we all know, Congress just isn't working. Sure, they *go* to work but they don't get anything done. I'm just sick of it and I'm certain you are, too.

"Believe me, I'm not a political person. I won't tell you whether I'm a registered Democrat or Republican because party label doesn't mean anything to me. I vote for the man, or the woman. I vote for who I think will work hard and represent me – us – well. And those who represent us in Congress should be ashamed of what they accomplish on our behalf."

His voice became more forceful. "The American public's approval rating of Congress is about as low as any time in history. What – mid-teens to 20 percent? Horrible. I'd be embarrassed if I were a congressman or senator but they've grown numb to criticism. The number of bills they pass each year is absurdly low."

Now Charlie was close to shouting. "Congress is comprised of men and women who serve their own interests. Too many are controlled by lobbyists. Neither party wants to work with the other, and within each party are liberals and conservatives who don't trust one another. Then there's the ultra-liberal Fig Leaf movement among the Democrats that only serves to add confusion. The parties can't agree on major issues ranging from immigration reform to the federal deficit. There's stagnation, and meaningful legislation doesn't get passed. Gridlock, nothing but gridlock. Taxpayers are throwing money away by funding chaos. When I see Congress basically doing nothing, it really makes me damned angry."

His closed right fist struck the top of the lectern so hard the jolt nearly knocked the microphone to the floor. The audience rose with such a rush two chairs were upended. Deafening applause and shout-outs filled the room, drowning out Charlie's "Pardon my language" apology.

"Give 'em hell, Simpson." "You're damned right." "You said it!"

As people began sitting, a voice from the right side of the room called out. "Charlie, let's do something about it." It was Omer Hardin.

Charlie wiped his eyes with the back of his right hand. "Thank you, Omer. We should, and this is what the four of us up here propose – that we businessmen and women launch a campaign to replace our congressman. If people elsewhere in Indiana and other states learn about this, perhaps they'll take similar action. We'll use different slogans such as Time for an Overhaul and Clean House (and Senate)." He displayed a slight smile as he thought of the cleverness of the latter. "It's time for massive changes."

Applause again.

Not everyone was in agreement. "Surely you don't think our effort in this little county will have any national impact," a man in the front row challenged.

"Perhaps it won't," Charlie responded, "but hopefully the two candidates who're running for the vacant senate seat from Indiana will take note and sharpen their thinking during the campaign and the election will give us a new congressman. And maybe, just maybe, people in other states will take notice of what we're doing if we can get the word out. I'm not an expert at how to do that but perhaps we can get the *Hopewell County Gazette* to run an article. I know nothing about how to use social media. If anyone here does, let me know."

"Wait just a minute," a man said as he rose from the middle of the third row. "Several of you know me. I'm Bill Phillips and I own a men's clothing store on the square in Pemberton. I think you – we – are moving a little too fast. Let's really think this through. We can't afford to have your proposed effort backfire on us. What if the public doesn't agree and takes it out on us by refusing to do business with us? I'll admit I'm a Democrat and I've supported the Democratic party all my adult life. I have a lot of friends who are strong party people. While I don't agree with all that Congressman

Wilburn's done, or not done, I don't know that he should to be voted out of office. The alternative could surely be worse. That's my two cents worth." He sat down.

"I'll respond to that," someone else said. She rose. "I'm Melany Coffin from Clyde and I own Cleavage Bar & Grill." There were a few chuckles. Looking over the room, the buxom blonde continued, "I'm a Democrat, too, and have lots of friends who are Democrats. Some of them would've voted a straight party ticket in the past even if one of their candidates was convicted of his third DUI the week before the election. But I sense a change in them. I hear lots of grousing from bar patrons, some of them the very friends I just mentioned. My two cents worth is that it's time for some drastic action."

Charlie thanked her for speaking up.

"This proposed campaign is not for everyone. But we four up here are so committed to the idea that we've prepared a statement and I'll read it."

Charlie took glasses from his shirt pocket and slipped them on, then picked up a sheet of paper.

> We, the undersigned owners and operators of small businesses in Hopewell County, have grown weary of years of inaction on needed legislation by the Congress of the United States. We feel the persons in whom American voters have placed their trust no longer deserve it. We hereby urge all registered voters to cast their ballots against our congressman who is running for re-election in the November 2016 election. It's time to start anew.

"We have several clipboards with this statement on it and space under the statement to sign your name if you so choose. If you sign, you're consenting to permit handbills and possibly newspaper advertisements to include your name. Handbills will be produced and delivered for you to display in your establishment's front window and any other place within the building.

"We will send you an envelope to use for any donation to the cause. The money will basically offset the costs of producing the printed materials. At this point, there are no plans for placing ads on the radio station in Pemberton.

"Is there anything anyone else wants to say?" He paused briefly. "If not, we'll adjourn and pass out the clipboards with the statement. The four of us thank all of you for coming tonight and voicing your opinions. The task ahead will not be easy but we can at least let Congress know we're more than unhappy with its lack of production. "

Charlie started to walk from the lectern as people began rising from their chairs, then he abruptly returned. "Oh, I forgot something very important. On behalf of the four of us, I want to make it clear that we will not – and we hope no one will – harbor any resentment toward those who don't sign the statement. We know this is a controversial move and there are very good reasons why some people will choose not to sign. We fully support their right to do so and expect to be good business neighbors regardless. I just wanted to be sure to make that point before we all leave. Thank you."

Around the room, people formed lines behind those holding clipboards, and voices filled the air. Later, Carnahan informed Charlie and the other two that she'd observed a few leaving immediately after the meeting and not signing. Charlie started counting the signatures on the sheets.

"How many were here, Charlie?" Jack Peterson asked.

Interrupted, Charlie held his finger at a spot on the list. "My wife said she counted 96 and that included two young people – possibly high school students with their parents." He continued his count.

"This is amazing." A broad smile covered his face. "If there were 94 business people here, all but nine signed the statement. That is amazing, fantastic."

Smiles filled their faces and Peterson and Carlson high-fived.

"Wow, this is indeed something special," Carnahan remarked. "I can't wait to hear reaction when it starts coming in in a few days. I just hope this doesn't backfire."

CHAPTER 7

Reaction didn't come in days – it was almost immediate. Noon the following day.

"Charlie, there's some guy on the phone who says he's with CBS News in Chicago. He wants to talk with you," called out Terry McKinney who'd answered and placed the phone call on hold, then found Charlie helping a customer load some bricks into a pickup behind the store.

Charlie looked dumbfounded. Handing his work gloves to McKinney, he said, "Here, take these and help Joe with the bricks," as he stepped into the store and headed to his office.

"Charlie Simpson," he said into the receiver.

"Mr. Simpson, this is Bill Roberts of CBS News in Chicago. I've just seen a video of you that's gone viral."

Charlie was taken aback. *What have I done wrong?* he wondered.

"What video?" Charlie replied.

"A video of you making an emotional speech to an audience last night. You got pretty passionate and what you proposed is spreading like wildfire on social media," Roberts said.

Charlie asked, "Who took the video? How'd you get it?"

"I don't know who took it but it must have been on an iPhone or iPad. Someone downloaded it to the internet and it's gone from YouTube to Facebook. Twitter is filled with reaction, and based on everything we've learned, it's being talked about around the country."

"You've got to be kidding," Charlie exclaimed. "We certainly didn't hire anyone to take video and if they did it was done secretly." He paused. "Not that it matters. We certainly want people everywhere to know what we're doing."

"I have a few questions for you, Mr. Simpson. Many would say that's a pretty bold campaign you've proposed. Do you really believe it will work?"

"I have no idea if it will," Charlie replied. "But it's something that nearly ninety small businessmen and women here in southwestern Indiana obviously feel strongly enough to put their names on a statement that's going to be displayed in their stores."

"Oh, you won't have to wait for that to be displayed, Mr. Simpson. People everywhere are finding out about it already. Aren't you afraid of backlash from this – that people will take it as you and the others being unpatriotic and undemocratic?"

"Not for one second," Charlie replied. "It's the democratic system for people to urge others to support or not support candidates. In fact, those of us behind this think it's unpatriotic and undemocratic for congressmen to take the American public's dollars and waste them by not acting on anything significant. Their actions are the very reason we think every one of them running for re-election should not be re-elected. They should be ashamed of themselves."

"Can I send a crew down to Jefferson to interview you tonight?"

Charlie gulped. "Tonight?"

"Yes, we've got a private jet standing by at O'Hare and would fly to Evansville, then drive up to meet you."

"Well, that's no problem for me. My store's open til 9 o'clock. Can they be here before then?"

"I suspect they'll get there by 7, if that's all right with you."

"OK. I'll see them then." Charlie thought for an instant. "Oh, should I invite the other three who helped me organize last night's meeting?"

"That'd be great. We'd love to talk with all four of you."

In between calling Mary Carnahan, Jack Peterson, and Jason Carlson – they agreed to meet at the hardware store at 6:30 – Charlie took seven calls from other media – *New York Times, Evansville Courier & Press, Indianapolis Star,* three radio stations, and a television station in Louisville. Shortly after 2 o'clock, reporters and cameramen from two Evansville TV stations showed up, unannounced.

Charlie's life had been turned upside down. Things would never be the same.

"Do you think you can be successful in getting a massive turnover in Congress?" reporter Skip Foster of WTVW asked. Lights glaring at him from near the checkout counter in the store, Charlie replied. "Honestly, while we're upset with all of Congress, our initial interest in organizing last night's meeting was to rally small business people behind an effort to not re-elect our own district congressman. But if attention is growing elsewhere, we'd welcome similar movements."

"Who's 'we?'"

"Initially the four of us local business owners who called for the meeting last night, but now dozens of county businesspeople who are behind the effort," Charlie answered.

Reporter Julie Anderson of WEHT in Evansville asked, "Do you plan to take this campaign to other southern Indiana counties?"

"No," Charlie said. "I plan to concentrate on my own county." He paused. "But if I can be of help to others, I'll be available."

Anderson followed, "Mr. Simpson, do you mean you want to see U.S. House Speaker David Flores out of office? He's been a mainstay for twenty years, half of it as speaker."

"I want to see all 435 representatives replaced," Charlie replied. "If Mr. Flores had been doing his job, he'd have found a way to break gridlocks and get the two parties in the House to pass more meaningful legislation. Sorry, Mr. Flores needs to go. And that applies to the leaders of both parties in the House and those that are up for reelection in the Senate. All of them."

Charlie surprised himself at enjoying being the center of attention and by his composure and occasional wit.

Business in the store had all but stopped, as customers, bystanders, and the two salespeople on duty stood and watched, intrigued by Charlie's sudden fame.

When the interviews concluded, Charlie was handed nearly a dozen pink WHILE YOU WERE OUT notes with reporter names and phone numbers. He quickly saw the day had turned into a disaster from the standpoint of getting hardware store business accomplished and asked Sarah to come in as a backup in case sales picked up, and to bring him a sandwich and a clean shirt before CBS got there.

He spent the next two hours talking on the phone and in person with reporters who kept asking the same questions he'd heard before. A third Evansville television station, WFIE, showed up and got a live interview at the beginning of its 5 o'clock newscast. Charlie managed to down the ham and cheese sandwich Sarah brought and changed shirts – a light blue one with *SIMPSON HARDWARE* imprinted in dark blue on the left side breast pocket – before his three business friends arrived to discuss what they might say or how they might respond to the CBS reporter's questions. Finally, at 7:10, the reporter and cameraman came in after taking video of the front of the store.

"Bernard Duffy," the reporter said as he held out his right hand to shake Charlie's. "Thanks for agreeing to talk with me."

"I don't mind at all," Charlie responded. "And I want you to meet the others who are in this with me." Charlie introduced them before Carnahan said, "The four of us organized last night's meeting but Charlie's our spokesman."

"I understand that, but if you don't mind, I'd like to interview all of you as a group. Is that okay?" Duffy asked.

Sarah helped Charlie arrange four chairs in a semi-circle, facing the photographer and Duffy. Lights attached to floor stands were placed front left and right and the light standards' barn doors were adjusted to illuminate the four to the cameraman's satisfaction. "I'm ready," he announced to Duffy who stood just to the side of the camera.

"Mr. Simpson, I'll start with you. As best you can, summarize the intent of your campaign."

Charlie responded as he had numerous times all afternoon.

"I understand that your initial intent was aimed at your district representative – Democratic Congressman Harold Wilburn – and the senate race in Indiana, but you've touched off something far, far bigger than your county. Are you prepared for all the attention your campaign is going to bring, some of it quite negative?" Duffy asked.

Charlie looked at the others, then to the camera, "I don't think any of us thought of something like this happening this quickly. But if the attention is going to result in something similar happening elsewhere, we'd be thrilled."

Carlson chimed in, although obviously nervous, "I, I agree with Charlie. We're owners of little businesses and we all work hard for a living. We're just four of the 'common people' of this country – just like millions of others. And there are things Congress should be doing to make lives better but we see nothing getting done. We're sick and tired of it and we suspect the American public is, too."

Carnahan nearly cut him off. "Sorry for the language, but we are damn mad. Damn mad at the lack of action in Washington. What's sad is that getting things done there shouldn't be that complicated. As one of our fellow business owners said to me, 'It ain't rocket science.'" She leaned back in her chair and folded her arms, proud of her fortitude and salty language.

Peterson sat still, frozen at the thought of being in front of a network reporter and camera.

"Well," Duffy said, "do you have any idea what a tall order it is to take on the entire Congress? There will be 435 House seats up for election this fall and it's almost June. Some current members are retiring and some are running for Senate seats. Certainly, you don't think all 435 seats will be held by newly-elected representatives in January?"

"But wouldn't it be great if at least half of them were new members?" Charlie responded. "Just think what a fresh start that would be. And if the current leadership was among those not re-elected, a whole lot of new blood could actually flow in. The electorate will have spoken and the message will be loud and clear – get something done and do it now!" Charlie's voice rose as he emphasized his final words.

"Let's look at the Senate," the reporter declared. "Approximately one-third of the one hundred seats will be up for grabs. Your senator in Indiana is retiring, so you won't have anyone to vote against. Who do you support among the two candidates?"

Finally, Peterson spoke up, and rapidly. "We don't care, as long as the person gets the message that Indiana voters are going to be looking closely at everything he or she does if they get elected and we'll do everything we can to make sure their time in office is only the allotted six years if they don't do a good job." Peterson swallowed hard, his hands death-gripping the sides of his chair so no one could see how nervous he was. "I suspect we'll see the winner working their tail off to try to get Congress to move into action starting in January."

The interview continued another thirty minutes, with all four getting opportunities to talk about what they wanted Congress to enact, how difficult it was to run a small business, and what their hopes were for the future of the country.

That night, in the darkness of their bedroom, Sarah lay beside her emotionally drained husband, an arm across his chest, and kissed him on the cheek. Softly, "I'm *so* proud of you – taking up a cause for all the common people. I'll support you in every way and take care of the store. Don't worry about it. You just do what you need to do. You're a good man, Charlie Simpson." She kissed him again. Sarah couldn't see it, but there was a faint beam to his face as Charlie drifted to sleep.

★★★★★

The following day, Charlie got nothing done business-wise. Sarah made certain customers were served. He fielded dozens of media telephone calls, including *The Telegraph* in London and *The Sydney Morning Herald* in Australia. Radio and television reporters stopped at the store unannounced. Mid-afternoon, a producer from NBC's Today Show called and set up an interview for the following morning. The bad news was Charlie had to be ready for the interview at 6 a.m., because Jefferson was an hour behind New York.

"Mr. Simpson, you've created quite a stir. You know that, don't you?" Maria Suarez asked from her anchor desk on the Today Show set.

"I'm certainly beginning to realize it," Charlie replied, seated on a bar stool in the middle of his store, surrounded by bright lights that not only illuminated him but some of the product aisles in the background. He felt calm. And confident. At home.

"Well, sir," Suarez continued, "in little more than a day you have caused a lot of people across the United States to discuss embarking on similar anti-Congress movements in their areas. What do you say to that?"

"First, I wouldn't describe what we are doing as 'anti-Congress,'" Charlie injected. "Congress is the lifeblood of this country, far more important than who is president. No matter what the president wants done, Congress makes the decisions. We are anti incumbents. The people in office get nothing meaningful accomplished and haven't for years. They need to be replaced."

"Mr. Simpson, do you actually think there is any chance for a turnover of that magnitude?"

"All I know, Ms. Suarez, is that if we take action and are successful in our congressional district and others do that in their districts throughout the U.S., the results might be quite astonishing. And important for our nation's future."

"Mr. Simpson, let's get to specifics. What exactly is it that you feel Congress has not been doing and needs to do?"

Sounding a bit sarcastic while not meaning to, Charlie replied, "I know that you know the answer to what Congress has not done but I'll give you the opinion of the owner of one small business. Tax laws are confusing and complex as they relate to small businesses. Tax rates are unfairly weighted against small businesses. Health care reform is needed to make it more possible for employees of small businesses like mine to get health insurance at affordable rates. The national debt needs to be pared. Online retailers need to be forced to collect sales taxes that states aren't getting. Full repeal of the estate tax. No one in Congress seems to have the bal.." he paused for the word, "the gumption to settle the immigration question. The list goes on and on.

"It just gripes me and other small business owners that American taxpayers are paying their elected officials to work on their behalf and what they are getting in return are a bunch of adults acting like little school children and refusing to get along with one another. What we need, instead, are elected federal officials who dedicate themselves to working together even when they don't agree on all the issues, compromise when necessary, and get legislation approved."

"But Mr. Simp….."

"Let me go even further," Charlie continued, "I think there should be discussions about abolishing both major political parties."

The camera in the New York studio showed an astonished network anchorwoman. "Abolishment of the Democratic and Republican parties?"

"Yes, ma'am, that's exactly what I'm saying," Charlie replied. "The current problem we have in this country – or at least at the heart of the problem – are politicians who vote as their party leaders dictate. Representation of the people has gone out the window. So, what we have are Republicans who refuse to get along with Democrats, and vice versa, and their leaders demand of all their members in Congress to do what they say. There's stalemate after stalemate.

"What we need is for people to run for office and get elected on what they believe as individuals and not on what some party tells them to do. Then if they don't do it when they're in office, voters can decide whether to give them another opportunity."

"But Mr. Simp......."

"Party platforms are meaningless," Charlie continued, hardly taking a breath. "All they do is tie the hands of people who need to be acting on behalf of their constituents and what their constituents want accomplished, not what some party controlled by lobbyists wants.

"I'll go further. I think it's unpatriotic for anyone to vote a straight ticket – straight Republican or straight Democrat. It is absolutely impossible for all of the candidates from any party to be worthy of representing their constituents. Voting all one party means being blind to what is good for the country." He stopped.

Suarez paused for a moment. "Mr. Simpson, you've certainly injected a major subject into the debate – eliminating the parties. It's a pretty radical idea, wouldn't you say?"

"Maybe," Charlie replied. "I just think it's something that would be good for the country, but it's an idea for future consideration, not today. The main thing now is to find better representation in Congress in this fall's elections."

★★★★★

Reaction to Charlie's comments was intense and immediate. He was assailed by the chairs of both major political parties. Congressmen and senators joined the reaction. "Lunatic" was one of the more kind references. He might as well have closed his store, because the onslaught of media was such that it was difficult for customers to enter the building or move through the aisles in search of an ax handle or garden hose.

Social media was abuzz, not all of it what Charlie would have wanted.

crazee2   The guy's nuts.

dement1   Replacing congressmen is one thing; eliminating parties is brainless.

Gregory44   Wonder what kind of businessman he is; stupid ideas.

Alize666   Yeah, someone needs to shut him up.

"Charlie, what in the world have you done? What were you thinking?" Sarah asked when she called him to their small office and closed the door. "Have you gone crazy?"

"Yeah, I know, I shouldn't have said that about the parties, but I believe it and it just came out of my mouth. There's nothing I can do about it now," he said.

"Well, there *is* something you can do, you can withdraw that remark with the next reporter who interviews you. You've just injected something that will be an enormous distraction from what you and the others want. It may be enough to defeat your whole original idea."

"I can't do that, Sarah," Charlie replied. "I've said it and I can't back down. What I *can* do is stop talking about it unless questioned, not make it a major point."

Coldly, Sarah countered, "Well, my dear, I think you may have sounded the death knell to what you wanted to achieve and I'm sorry for you. By tomorrow morning, you might be the laughing stock of the nation."

Going to his truck behind the store, Charlie found all four tires flat. "Watch out" was spray-painted black across the windshield. He called Jefferson police and an incident report was taken. It was the first time Charlie'd felt unnerved by his stance.

★★★★★

He hardly slept that night, tossing and turning, fearing he had undermined what he and his three Jefferson business friends wanted to achieve and earned their wrath in return.

His phone rang at 6 a.m. "Charlie, sorry if I woke you but you gotta tune into Good Morning America. They're going to have a report you'll wanta see." Groggy, Charlie recognized Jason Carlson's voice, mumbled something, crawled from bed, and went into the living room where he turned on the television and heard "We get this report from ABC national political correspondent Tanya Bayliss."

"Hi, Logan. That little group of business owners in the Hoosier state – whether they intended to or not – has certainly gotten the attention of the parties and leaders in Congress. Thanks to the global, rapid-fire impact of social media, the effort launched by the owners in Hopewell County, Indiana, has created an overnight national reaction that has turned into national action."

Charlie watched as Bayliss continued speaking while video showed rallies from several sites.

"Last night, in cities and small towns across the nation, groups held special meetings to begin organizing what are definitely anti-incumbent efforts. People are jumping on the bandwagon and the expectation is that this could spread to campaigns everywhere.

"In Avondale, Arizona, for example, owners of small businesses banded together for the first time, to launch a move against their district's incumbent congressman. Bud Turner was a spokesman for the group."

"Like our fellow business owners in Indiana, we're fed up with congressional inaction and we agree a change is needed," Turner said to an assemblage of reporters.

"In North Platte, Nebraska, a similar rally, and the same in Aiken, South Carolina."

Now back on camera, Bayliss said, "Logan, I've talked with people within the leadership of both major parties and they're concerned. They lashed out at the Indiana hardware store owner who proposed yesterday that their parties be eliminated, but I can tell you they know that's a side issue for the time being. The big issue is what appears to be a quickly growing movement in this country and that is an effort to oust every incumbent in Congress. It is a troubling matter for them, indeed."

★★★★★

"Mr. Simpson," the caller said right after Charlie answered the phone in his office later that Saturday morning. "This is Harold Wilburn." Charlie instantly recognized his congressman's name.

"I'd love to meet with you Mr. Simpson and discuss your concerns about Washington and what I've been trying to do about it."

A smirk hit Charlie's face but he decided not to convey the attitude in the tone of his voice. "Well, thank you for calling, Congressman. I'll be glad to talk with you anytime. But let me say that I've followed you pretty well in the media throughout your time in office and I don't ever recall reading or hearing that you've done anything to try to get both parties to work together. I don't recall you ever having a town meeting here in Jefferson to hear your constituents on any issues that are on their minds. I don't recall you attending any event here in Jefferson to show that you have any interest in anything in this town."

"Well, Mr. Simp....."

"So, as for meeting with me now that I have raised some serious concerns about you and others in Congress, I'm not certain it would do any good, but I'm not closed-minded to talking with you."

They agreed the ball was in Charlie's court as to when he would want to get together. He promised a return call.

As Charlie and the congressman were talking, two men huddled in a booth in the back of a nondescript neighborhood restaurant in Washington, D.C.

"That son-of-a-bitch has got to be taught a lesson. The fear of God's got to be put in him. You understand?" the 40ish dark-haired man in a business suit said in a low but harsh voice while leaning on his elbows and addressing the ruddy-faced, casually-dressed, older man across the table.

"I got it, but does The Man agree with this?" he inquired quietly, never taking his eyes off the other.

"The Man wants this done, you got it?"

"I got it. With my contacts, it won't take long to get the job done."

"You live in a world that's dark."

Four days later, in the middle of the afternoon, two men strode to the small parking area behind Charlie's store. While one kept a lookout, the other quickly planted a small device under the front left wheel well of Charlie's pickup truck. They left without being noticed. They thought.

★★★★★

The phone rang.

"Yeah," the terse answer.

"What the hell's taking so long?" the agitated caller questioned.

"Hey, you asked me to get a job done and I'll do it. Give me enough credit to know I don't want to screw this up. The guys planted a GPS under the pickup. We wanna follow his daily movements so we don't make a mistake."

"Well, The Man's anxious. This guy's getting way too much attention. He needs a little scare."

Irritated, the older man from the restaurant meeting replied sarcastically. "You tell *The Man* that nothing will happen for two weeks at minimum – maybe three – but when it's done it'll be done right. That's the way we do things in my profession. *OK?*"

"You got five days, no ifs, ands, or buts."

"Sorry, no promises. This is on my timeline."

Furious, the caller pushed the end-call button on his iPhone.

★★★★★

Charlie continued getting daily media calls and was thankful for Sarah working full-time at the store. Sales were up, thanks in part to out-of-towners who stopped to see the newly famous owner. What they didn't see was the word "Pig" spray-painted in red on a rear window when Charlie arrived for work one morning. It took him fifteen minutes to remove it with paint thinner and he never told Sarah.

Later that morning, he got a phone call. "Remember Elmer Clifton?" the muffled voice said.

"Who is this?" Charlie responded.

"Don't matter none. Just always look behind you and be aware of someone lurking." The line went dead.

Charlie was shaken. He hadn't heard Elmer Clifton's name in over thirty years. He and Sarah had tried so hard to put that face behind them. He didn't tell anyone about the call.

CHAPTER

8

"Charlie, I've sent out notices for the next county business owners meeting, just like we'd discussed," Jack Peterson reported when the two met in Charlie's office. "I think we'll have a big crowd, and we have to decide whether to allow the media to be there."

"We've got no choice, Jack. We need all the attention we can get and even though we've got to talk more strategy, it won't hurt to do it in public."

Peterson cleared his throat and searched for words. Charlie frowned.

"It's really interesting, Charlie. Some of us thought you'd stepped on your dick when you brought up abolishing political parties in that interview. We thought you, and we, would become laughing stocks because of what some still think is a harebrained idea. But, you know what," – Peterson wasn't requesting a response – "…it hasn't hurt us one bit as far as we can tell. Most of us – well, all those I've talked to – haven't seen any drop in our business. Sure, we've had people cuss us, tell us we're unpatriotic, tell us we have no business organizing against our congressman, and say 'I'll never do business with you again.' I know two businesses in Pemberton that have had problems – someone set fire to materials in a dumpster behind one of the stores and someone painted "Pig" in big letters on the front windows of another." Charlie grimaced but said nothing. "But overall, Charlie, support for what we're doing has been strong."

"I like the 'support' part, Jack, but I sure as hell don't like the other. We've really stirred things up, haven't we?"

"I'll say."

"I've been too busy to notice, have you been interviewed by the media?" Charlie asked.

"Have I? Nothing like you, but plenty to take me away from getting things done. The same with Mary and Jason."

"Be prepared," Charlie responded. "I suspect it'll get worse as time goes along, especially when we all meet next week."

"What's a little disappointing," Peterson said, "is the amount of organizing I've read about in the country isn't as strong as I'd suspected it might be."

"Give it time," Charlie replied. "These things take time." He paused. "I never knew much about social media but, boy, can it ever be strong. I was blown away by what happened after our initial get together. Wait 'til next week, and if someone records our meeting on their iPhone, iPad, or whatever else people use these days, I'm guessing it'll go viral – I think that's the term they use – and there'll be even more interest in our plan."

★★★★★

"Sarah, can you go get a load of clay tile tomorrow morning?" Charlie asked. It was two days before the scheduled business owners' meeting at the Business Development Office in Pemberton. "Jeff Clark's working on a drainage project at his farm and needs tile tomorrow afternoon. I'm going to be tied up with another TV reporter who's coming to the store. Tried to delay it, but she said she wants to make the noon news. I'll have the truck gassed up for you."

"Sure enough, hon. I assume the guys in Evansville will load the tile for me."

"No, they expect the buyer to do all the work," he said, looking serious. Then he burst out laughing.

"Oh, Charlie." She punched him lightly on the upper arm.

While Sarah slept that evening, Charlie lay on his side, listening to her steady, low breathing, and thinking of how happy he was. Sarah had become such a wonderful woman. The assault more than thirty years ago had tormented her, he knew, although they'd seldom needed to talk about it. The only good that came from it, in his mind, was she began looking at life differently after that, at the positives and possibilities and not so much of life being negative. She knew she was lucky – they both were, in fact – to be alive. Their marriage had experienced its challenges, but they were deeply in love.

As he fell asleep, two figures stepped out of the shadows and headed toward the metal and fiberglass carport beside the house.

★★★★★

Charlie awoke before Sarah, showered, quickly drank coffee that had brewed when the automatic digital timer on the machine displayed 6:00, and was in the Malibu on his way to the store just before 7. They lived just six blocks away.

Knowing she didn't have to be in Evansville until 10, Sarah enjoyed a leisurely early morning, staying in bed until 7:45, standing in the hot shower for what seemed like an eternity, eating her typical light breakfast of whole wheat toast and Greek fruit yogurt, and then leaving the house for the forty-five-minute drive to the drain pipe distributor in Evansville. The sky was cloudless and

Sarah could sense the June day would be warm and humid, a little more than normal for late spring in southwestern Indiana.

She didn't drive the two-year-old Ford F-150 often but enjoyed its ride when she did. Stepping into the vehicle and sliding behind the wheel, Sarah placed her purse on the passenger side of the seat, adjusted the rearview and side mirrors, inserted the ignition key and turned it.

The coroner later said Sarah was unconscious before the fire consumed her.

The explosion was heard in downtown Jefferson. Charlie heard it, sitting in his store office. Terry McKinney rushed to the back door.

"Charlie," he yelled, "There's thick smoke in the direction of your neighborhood!"

Charlie bolted from his chair and ran to McKinney's vantage point. "Oh, my God!"

Charlie rushed out the door and to his car, hearing sirens as he reached the driver's side. The engine wouldn't turn over. *This can't be. Not now!* The car started. By the time he turned the corner of Elm and Seventh streets and saw two fire trucks and a police cruiser, fear overcame him. He assumed it was his house. He found it was worse.

Foam was being poured onto flames that had engulfed the twisted metal of Charlie's pickup.

"Sarah, Sarah," he screamed as he rushed up the driveway toward the wreckage, then quickly veered to the side door of the house. "Sarah, Sarah," he yelled as he struggled to unlock the door, then rushed inside. "Sarah, are you in here?" he screamed in a panic-driven frenzy, eyes darting into the living room as he moved through the hallway to the bedrooms. "Sarah, are you here?" Charlie wheeled and headed back toward what had been the carport.

The flames were now extinguished. Firemen surrounded the blackened metal and one of them turned in time to grab Charlie as he burst toward them. "Whoa, whoa. You live here?" he asked as Charlie tried to wrestle away.

Charlie screamed, "Yes, God dammit. Let go of me."

Another fireman recognized him. "You don't want to look in there. Believe me, Mr. Simpson, you don't want to look in there," he pleaded, finally unable to restrain Charlie.

Charlie wrestled free, moved two steps toward the truck, and suddenly stopped – the badly burned body only four feet away.

"Sarah?" he yelled at the fireman. "Is that my wife?"

Two firemen were quickly at his side, each with hands around his biceps, restraining him.

"I'm sorry, sir, we don't know if it's a man or woman. The metal's far too hot to touch anything."

When he awoke in Hopewell County Hospital in Pemberton, Charlie was told he'd passed out two hours earlier after yelling Sarah's name uncontrollably for as much as a minute. Heavily sedated and lying in the bed, he remembered none of it. He was handed a gold wedding band.

"Charlie, I'm deeply, deeply sorry, if that's your wife's." Charlie recognized Jefferson police chief Larry Miles. "We found the ring in the area of the front seat. If it's hers, it still doesn't mean she was the person in the truck. It may be someone else. We can't be certain. But we know it was a female."

An Act of Frustration

Charlie began whimpering, staring at the ring in the palm of his right hand. Miles continued. "We've called in Indiana State Police because we don't know, and don't have the expertise to know, what caused the explosion. Neither does the county sheriff's department. The federal Bureau of Alcohol, Tobacco, Firearms, and Explosives will also be involved. The ATF investigates all explosions." The sound from Charlie's mouth became a low-level but shrill cry which only a violin could mimic in the upper reaches of the *E*-string as he looked out over the foot of the bed, clutching the ring in a closed fist.

"I promise you this, Charlie, we *will* get to the bottom of this and as quickly as possible," Miles continued.

"I want to introduce you to Detective James Sturgis of the state police. He's been assigned responsibility for this case." Tears flowing down his face, Charlie glanced at the trooper, then dropped his head again.

"Mr. Simpson, my specialty is investigating explosions," Sturgis explained. He continued in a somewhat compassionate, yet matter of fact tone. "Typically, causes of blasts are not quickly determined. In this situation, since a person was in the vehicle, we must consider homicide, whether this may have been intentional." Charlie's head shot up, his eyes widened.

"Homicide? Murder? You think someone killed Sarah?"

"Sir, it's standard operating procedure when a body, er, a, human being is a victim," Sturgis responded. "I'll have a team of experts assisting me and we'll move as quickly but as carefully as possible to ascertain the cause of the explosion. Meanwhile, the county coroner will determine the identity of the person who was in the truck." Sturgis allowed Charlie time to absorb what he'd just said. "Sir, I need to ask two questions, if you don't mind. Do you know why your wife would be driving your truck this morning and are you aware of anyone who might have wanted to bring harm to you or your wife?"

Charlie made a low, mournful sound. His head hung. The officers said nothing.

Attempting to compose himself, and interrupting his words with staccato sobs, Charlie explained that he always drove the pickup but had asked Sarah to take it to Evansville for a load of tile because he'd become so popular the media wouldn't leave him alone.

The scheduled interview with a reporter spared his life and took Sarah's. He was on the verge of completely losing his emotions.

Sturgis's left eyebrow rose as he glanced toward Chief Miles. "So you *always* drove the truck?" the trooper asked.

Struggling to make words, Charlie replied softly, "Well, ninety-nine percent of the time."

"And yet today you asked her to?" Sturgis queried, sounding suspicious.

"Well, yes, last night," Charlie stated, a frown showing above his reddened eyes. "Why such questions?"

"Oh, there's no particular meaning to them, sir, other than to establish some base line information." The detective paused. "As to the other question, sir, do you know of anyone who would want to harm you or your wife?"

Charlie recalled the threatening phone call that asked if he remembered Elmer Clifton. It had been on his mind daily. He related it and the attempted rape of Sarah to the officers.

"Have you received similar calls or been the target of any violence?"

Charlie's mind was too cloudy to recall the flattened tires and spray paint on his truck or "Pig" on the back store window. "No. No."

"We'll leave you to rest, Mr. Simpson, but if the doctors give clearance in a couple of hours, I'd like to visit with you again. It's important that we develop as much information as possible as quickly as we can. Time can be of the essence especially if we're dealing with a homicide. I'm certain you understand."

Charlie nodded.

"We might be dealing with someone who thought *Mr.* Simpson would be in that truck this morning, not his wife," Sturgis said to Miles as they left. "We have to move quickly. I'll put a guard on his room."

★★★★★

"You son-of-a-bitch. You god-damned son-of-a-bitch. I told you to scare him, not kill his wife! You bastards. All three of you!" The two men sat hunched over drinks at the same restaurant booth where their plan was hatched three-and-a-half-weeks earlier. With jaw set and teeth clinched, the younger vented his anger in a gruff tone low enough for other patrons not to hear. Leaning over the table, "What the fuck were you doing? I can tell you The Man is gravely concerned about this and my ass is now on the line."

Holding his open right palm toward the aggressor, the older man responded in an equally low, forceful voice. "Now wait a minute. Just wait a minute. Sources led me to two brothers who were highly recommended. They knew that area of Indiana and were chomping at the bit to get involved because for over thirty years they'd hoped for a chance to harm Mr. Simpson. The GPS device clearly showed Simpson's truck took the same route to work and home every day. They knew he was the one who drove the truck and they allowed plenty of time to get a perfect pattern on him, so how the hell were they to know that on this day the wife would drive it?"

"They wouldn't but they sure as hell didn't have to kill whoever drove the goddamned truck, you asshole."

"Obviously, they screwed up, and big time, I admit," he responded as he looked around to ensure no one was listening. "They were supposed to be experts at explosives and were given clear instructions to plant something that would cause damage but not hurt anyone. Unfortunately, whatever they did resulted in the lady being killed."

"Tell me about their interest in a vendetta."

"First, gotta share this with you. One of the dumbass brothers couldn't resist, so he calls Simpson on the phone at his store recently and threatens him – even refers to the old man who was killed when he tried to rape Simpson's girlfriend. The brother said he called anonymously – put a handkerchief over the mouthpiece. No doubt the FBI knows about that phone call already.

"Anyway, they told me Simpson killed their old man when he tried to rape Mrs. Simpson before the two were married. Their view has been that if the dad had just been caught and convicted, he'd be out of prison by now. No doubt their pent-up anger caused them to add more explosive than I wanted, and they probably planted it under the wrong area of the truck."

The younger man shook his head back and forth as he looked at the table, then said, "OK, here's what you're going to do. Get those bastards out of the country. Get them a one-way ticket to anywhere. I don't care if it's Timbuktu. Tell them to lay low until they hear from you again, but it might be months from now. Give 'em enough cash to live on and tell them more will be on its way after you know where they've settled. And for God's sake, tell them to keep their mouths shut. I've got a gut feeling the feds *will* get involved in this. If anything is tied back to The Man, we'll all be in a shit load of hurt."

★★★★★

Within two hours of Sarah's death, news of it began spreading through the country. Media descended on Jefferson and television cameras were set up in the street outside Charlie's house. Fearing Charlie had been the target of the bomb, Chief Miles decided to keep a squad car in front of the house twenty-four hours a day. The patrolman's presence had the effect of keeping media away as well. Charlie was grateful.

The business owners' meeting scheduled for Pemberton was postponed. Not surprisingly, some of the owners removed anti-incumbent placards from their premises, fearing physical harm themselves. Others took another tact, taking up the cause when they'd been on the sidelines in the past, and placed placards in their store windows in solidarity with the cause.

Social media was alive with news about the murder and a wave of protests in the form of anti-incumbent organizing efforts began building across the country. Whoever meant to scare Charlie, created more than they'd ever imagined. The political parties and all incumbents in the nation's capital were in for the fight of their lives.

Charlie didn't want to live or spend a minute thinking about politics. Alone in his home after being released from the hospital and driven to his side door by the sheriff in late afternoon, he alternately blamed God and himself – sometimes both – for Sarah's death, shouting and crying at the same time. He hurled two vases of condolence carnations against the living room walls. Charlie could have cared less about the water, broken glass, and strewn flowers. He knew Sarah was an innocent and unintended victim. "Why couldn't it have been me? Not my wonderful wife? She had nothing to do with what we were doing. Oh, God, why? Why?" Then his mood would turn to anger. "Come get me, you mother-fucker, whoever you are. Come here and I'll blow your god-damned head off. You mother-fucking bastard who picked on a good, kind woman. Your day in Hell is coming. I guarantee it!"

Charlie had told Dick Jones to close the store and put a 'CLOSED UNTIL FURTHER NOTICE' sign in the window. He promised employees would be paid during the closure.

Friends came by his house to check on him. They understood his disheveled look. Jerry Tevault swept up the flowers and shards of glass from the hardwood floor without asking how they got there. When his closest friend finished, Charlie mumbled, "Sorry 'bout that. Lost my head. You're a great friend, Jerry. Thanks."

Although Charlie and Sarah weren't members of any church, the United Methodist and Church of Christ congregations made certain he had all the food he would need, with people dropping by daily to bring casseroles and desserts. With everyone, he tried to express his appreciation but knew he didn't do a good job. He was lifeless. And guilt-ridden. He began toying with the idea of giving up the campaign that had consumed so much of him and likely killed Sarah.

There was a private graveside service, no funeral, no calling. Charlie, the few family members that he and Sarah had, his employees, and his and Sarah's closest friends attended.

★★★★★

The coroner's report stated that an explosion of unknown origin ripped through the floorboard under Sarah's feet with such force it blew off both legs beneath the knees. She had not engaged her seatbelt and her skull was deeply fractured when it struck the roof of the cab. The concussion rendered her unconscious immediately. Fire soon enveloped her and was the cause of death. The only solace Charlie received to ease the horrific thought of Sarah dying by fire was the coroner's comment that she probably would not have survived the devastating injuries suffered in the blast itself.

State police said its initial investigation showed a device containing metal and an unknown explosive material likely had been attached to the driver's underside frame of the truck and was set to discharge as soon as the ignition switch was activated. The blast ruptured the fuel line from a tank Charlie had filled the previous evening. Fire roared through the pickup. Sarah was dead before firemen could reach the scene. The carport had been destroyed and paint on the side of the house facing it was singed but otherwise damage was contained to the truck. With little evidence to point the blame at anyone, the department urged citizens to come forward with knowledge of any suspicious people or incidents they may have seen in Jefferson in the previous weeks.

CHAPTER 9

Two men dressed in business suits approached Charlie's house. It was the sixth afternoon since Sarah's death. They knocked, then went in.

"Mr. Simpson," State Police Detective Sturgis said, "this is agent Anthony Costelanto of the ATF. Agent Costelanto has been brought in as the lead investigator in your wife's murder. Our agency and local police are cooperating with him and have made him aware of all evidence we've gathered in the past week. The FBI is also involved."

"FBI?" Charlie queried, puzzled.

"Yes, sir," Costelanto answered. "The FBI will be involved unless it finds the act was not tied to terrorism.'" He allowed the news to sink in.

"Do the names Austin and Jeremiah Clifton mean anything to you?"

Charlie thought for a moment. "Can't say they do."

"Both are coal miners in southern Montana, sons of Elmer Clifton."

Charlie swallowed hard. That name again. He shuddered.

"Could one of them have been the guy who threatened me on the phone recently?" Charlie asked.

"Can't say; I mean, we don't know. We're looking into every angle possible."

Charlie inquired about progress.

"With all due respect, sir, we don't divulge much about our investigations but I promise to let you know if anything substantive develops."

Costelanto paused. "Mr. Simpson, I know you were quizzed at length before being released from the hospital, but I have a few more questions."

Charlie looked puzzled. "Am I a suspect?"

"We have no reason to believe you are, sir, but it would help if you cleared up a couple of things, if you don't mind."

"Goodness, I don't mind."

"Were you and your wife having any problems – marital problems, that is?"

Thrown off by the question, Charlie replied, "Well, Lord, no. Absolutely not. We were quite in love and worked our tails off to make a living. Times were often tough for us but other than disagree on inventory issues – whether to carry more or less of something – we had no problems in our marriage."

"Was she aware of your affair?"

Charlie's breathing stopped. He sat there, staring directly at Costelanto. Then he felt anger beginning to rise. "How dare you bring up something that happened more than twenty years ago as though it had any bearing on the fact that some son-of-a-bitch blew the hell out of my wife? Damn you….*sir*," emphasizing the final word with sarcasm. The veins in Charlie's neck were clearly visible and his face was growing red. "And to answer your question, yes, she knew. She knew because I told her. And because you probably want to know more, the one night in question was at a time when my wife was having recurring nightmares about the assault in 1982 and wasn't interested in sex. But I had to find out if our lack of togetherness was that or whether I was no longer attractive to women. I satisfied my question in that one evening and although Sarah had difficulty forgiving me, she did and we had a wonderful relationship and marriage until some bastard ended it several days ago. Now, does that answer your improper delving into my life?" he questioned with more sarcasm. "I could give you time, date, motel, and anything else you need but I assume you already have all of that. Maybe video, too!"

The agent didn't flinch – a seasoned interrogator.

"Mr. Simpson, my job is not to anger you for some frivolous reason. My job is to get to the facts of who killed your wife. Who would have wanted you dead? Or your wife dead? A disgruntled customer? A business owner who disagrees with your campaign? An ordinary citizen who took exception to what you are doing? A politician? We're looking at all angles. And I can't get to a final determination until I've eliminated every question that arises. If I've insulted you, I apologize, but there's no way to inquire about sensitive matters without posing questions.

"You may find it difficult to accept that we have to look at everyone who possibly had a grudge against your wife, or you. Always, the spouse of a murder victim is high on the list of people to interview. By your own admission, you asked your wife to sub for you and drive to Evansville. She was killed. We regret her death and we regret having to ask difficult questions of you. I hope you can understand and accept that."

Charlie sat there, looked at the floor, then at Costelanto. "I'm sorry," he said softly. "I understand why you're asking and all I want is for you to do your job and find the killer."

CHAPTER
10

The following morning, there was a development. "We may have gotten a break in the case, from security outside the supermarket catty-corner from the front of the Simpson store and possibly from a teenager's iPhone."

State Police Detective Sturgis made the opening comment at a status meeting with Costelanto and two fellow ATF agents who were joining the investigation.

"A teen?" agent Wayne Bennett responded.

"Yes, sir," Sturgis injected. "First, state police sought security videos from any stores near Simpson's. We started acting on this within four hours of Mrs. Simpson's death. A team of officers viewed video recordings from the day of the business owners' meeting until the moment of our requests. It was our luck that one of the outdoor cameras on the grocery showed two men acting somewhat suspicious as they walked to the rear parking area at the hardware store on May 25, twenty days before the truck explosion. One of them acted nonchalant but appeared to be on the lookout while the other disappeared from view. Only moments later, the other reappeared, each of them surveyed the area apparently to make certain no one was watching, then they walked west to what we assume was their car parked nearby.

"What is surprising is that instead of driving away and not coming close to the store, they drove up the street beside it, stopped at the stop sign, then turned south onto Main and presumably out of town. Their car drove out of camera view. Obviously, actions that weren't those of professionals.

"What they didn't know – or if they did, they ignored the fact – was that a group of teens had gathered on the sidewalk outside the community center just down the street from the hardware store and one of them was taking video of some of his friends as the car stopped at the sign, turned, and headed past them. The vehicle and its occupants were clearly visible in the video, although it has taken our lab a lot of hours to enhance the images in the front seat. The best view of them is pretty fleet. But it's better than anything we could get from the supermarket video.

"When word went out that we were looking for any videos of the area during a multiple-day period, the teen recalled the car – a late model, shiny blue BMW 340 – in his iPhone recording and his father contacted us. Turns out the kid's a car buff and that one caught his eye, stayed in his memory.

"To say the least, the boy and his father are scared to death. We won't reveal the video until necessary to do so and we'll protect the identity of the person who took it. The teen and his parents sure as hell aren't going to utter a word."

When Sturgis ended his revelations, Costelanto took over. "Based on the image of the two men in the car, the ATF has used its massive data files and found what we believe are the pair. We're working feverously to find them. If it's them, they have indirect ties to Charlie Simpson and his wife. Their arrest records are the length of your arm," he pointed to Bennett. "Let me caution, however, that we have no evidence that ties them directly to the death. We want them for questioning. It's the best lead we have.

"Their family connection with the Simpsons goes back to 1982 when their dad died while trying to rape Mrs. Simpson in the barn loft on her family's farm here in southern Indiana. She wasn't Mrs. Simpson then. They were dating at the time and having sex when a guy named Elmer Clifton assaulted both of them. He was killed when he fell from the loft during a scuffle with Mr. Simpson.

"We know from interviewing people that Clifton's two sons vowed revenge. They're about as worthless as their dad except that he was an unemployed drifter – a petty thief – at the time, and to their credit, they have jobs. Both live in northern Wyoming and work in explosives at a Montana coal mine just across the state line.

"Our investigation has found these two flew commercially from Billings, Montana, to Evansville and back on at least two occasions in a three-week period. We know that twice they rented a car, one of which matches the description of the one in the videos. What we don't know is where they are. The Montana mining company says they've failed to show up to work for more than a week.

"Interesting, isn't it, that if they'd rented a regular car – not a specialty one – their presence in the boy's video would've likely gone unnoticed?" Head nods and facial expressions reflected how bewildering the suspects' actions were.

"If their intent was to harm *Mr.* Simpson, they might try again, as foolish as that might seem. As you all know, dangerous men are not afraid to do what common sense people would consider pretty stupid and risky. So," pointing to the two agents, "we're going to give Mr. Simpson protection at all times. I want you to develop the schedule and you can rely on state and town police to assist you. I've got a commitment from Detective Sturgis and the Jefferson police chief. I want one officer near the home at all times, although not necessarily in uniform, and I want someone on duty in the store, perhaps as a janitor. I'll leave it to you two to work out.

"There's one more thing," Costelanto stated. "Besides not knowing the whereabouts of the two men we want for questioning, we don't know who they were working for. That's the other major part of what we've got to find out."

★★★★★

The following afternoon, Charlie addressed the ever present media in front of his home. He appealed for some privacy, but knew he'd never get it completely.

Surrounded by reporters as he stopped near the end of the concrete walkway leading from the front door, Charlie spoke from his heart, no notes or script: "I want to thank all those from Jefferson and everywhere who've expressed their sentiments to me this past week. I'm not certain how I'd have made it without such great support.

"I've had a lot of time to think while dealing with grief. I seriously considered dropping out of the effort to change the membership in Congress. After all, my wife is dead and until I learn otherwise, I'll believe it was because I was involved in the campaign. I've met with those who worked with me in launching the effort, and with others. They have been persuasive. I have a lot of emotional healing to do, but I will go forward. I'm convinced Sarah would want me to continue the fight.

"I'll consider Sarah the martyr in this movement, an incredibly loving, compassionate woman who was the innocent victim of a despicable, violent act." Charlie's eyes welled with tears and he paused, glanced down as he cleared his throat, then looked at the reporters and continued. "I will reopen my store tomorrow. I will ask that the media allow me some room and not come into the store to interview me or badger customers." He paused but a moment. "Sometimes I think reporters don't understand what a person has to deal with when they've suffered a horrible tragedy and loss in their lives. I hope you will understand my situation and focus on the investigation. And I welcome your reporting on our continuing campaign to oust the incumbents. I trust you will honor the line between public life and private life."

Charlie turned and walked back to the house. He took no questions despite the media clamor. "What about the investigation, Mr. Simpson? Are you cooperating?" "Have you been told of any suspects?" "What was your first reaction to your wife's death?" The litany continued as Charlie closed the door behind him.

★★★★★

Little was accomplished the day Charlie reopened the store. It wasn't due to being hounded by media but by dozens of well-wishers – friends, fellow business owners, customers. Dick and Terry, assisted by two part-time employees, handled the transactions and were buoyed by the outpouring of compassion that clearly strengthened their boss who was at times weepy, smiling, and somber. It had been over a week since Sarah was killed, and Charlie was on the road back. He must look ahead.

★★★★★

The small-business-owners rally in Pemberton brought more than three dozen reporters — national and local – all confined to an area cordoned off in the back of the large meeting room. The size of crowd had been anticipated, so the meeting site had been changed to accommodate everyone. It had been almost two-and-a-half weeks since Sarah's murder.

"I want to thank the American Legion post for permitting us to use this banquet hall," Jason Carlson began. "The Legion represents men and women who have fought to preserve freedom in this world and we – all of us assembled – represent men and women fighting to preserve our nation.

"As you know, this meeting was postponed due to a horrible incident. There are many of us in this room who suspect the culprit was someone who wants us to shut up, and an innocent, wonderful woman was the logic-defying victim. Of course, we don't know for *certain* that the incident was tied to politics, but if it was, let this be a warning that no one will shut us up – absolutely no one!" The audience of approximately 150 – some standing along the sides of the room – burst into applause.

"Without further ado," Carlson said, "please welcome the courageous man who launched the mission we will continue to fight – Charlie Simpson."

With that, except for the man with a cast on his left leg who sat on one end of the front row, everyone was standing and giving Charlie resounding applause. He didn't smile as he walked from his folding chair behind the lectern or as he stood for a few moments to nod lightly over and over, looking from one side of the room to the other, his eyes misty, gathering in the support and compassion of the moment. Charlie held up his hands to quiet the applause, but it continued until he finally began speaking. Slowly, audience members sat down.

"You have no idea what you have just said to me with your hands and I thank you from the bottom of my heart," he began, pausing, and surveying the crowd.

"The last seventeen days have been hell but your spirit has returned me to earth tonight. Thank you."

More applause.

"I won't speculate on Sarah's death. I trust in law enforcement to find who's responsible and whether he, she, or they were working for some *one* or some entity. I am dedicated to continuing our mission. Our work must go on." Deafening applause. "We want change in Washington and we have to be pleased with similar efforts that are under way elsewhere in the nation. But our work is here at home, here in our district. We want Congressman Wilburn defeated and we want Indiana's U.S. Senate candidates to know that we'll be watching their every word and every statement as they seek to replace our retiring senator. And, certainly, we hope those running for the state legislature from our area understand that we'll be highly interested in their words and actions as well." Applause again.

Charlie looked directly into eyes as the room grew quiet. "I realize not every small business owner in our county is behind this effort. Some just don't believe in what we're doing. Some do but are afraid of the risk – the possible loss of business or, now, physical harm. Of course, I realize some of you have had veiled threats if not actual ones. Not for one second would I say anything against those who are not involved in this effort and I hope you will follow my lead in this. For all of you who do support this movement, thank you for placing the campaign placards in your storefronts and for having the fortitude to deal with anyone who has expressed opposition to what you are doing. I admire you and respect you. We are on the right path.

"We've developed small sheets of information that you may place on your checkout counters or elsewhere in your businesses. These tell why Congress needs an overhaul."

"Charlie, Jim Mayer from Barclay," the man stated as he rose from his seat near the middle of the room, interrupting Charlie's remarks. "I need some advice – not that you're asking for any questions – but what if customers become argumentative with me in front of other customers? I had it happen the other day and almost had to call my town marshal but the guy suddenly turned and walked out the door. I was trying to calm him down and make my point but all he wanted to do was rant. I might have lost him as a customer, but I wasn't going to back down." Mayer sat down.

"Sounds like you handled that well," Charlie responded. "Do your best to get such a customer to go to your office and away from the earshot of others and let him say whatever he wants. Hopefully, people like that will at least listen to you and respect you for taking a stand. You can't let them disrupt your business."

One by one, several others raised questions on campaign issues, customer relations, and how to deal with the media. After just over an hour of dialogue – with some in the audience giving advice to others – Charlie wrapped up the meeting.

"We've had a good exchange tonight and I thank all of you who asked questions, those who gave advice, and those who listened. Those of you who came to listen as you make up your mind on whether to be part of this effort, thank you for attending. If I can ever be of assistance, please call on me. We're involved in an effort that might result in something dramatic nationally, but the main thing is we want to be successful in our congressional district. Urge your customers to vote in November.

"You may be sought out by media as you leave tonight. Your story – our story – is a good one and be glad there is interest in it being told.

"Good luck to us all."

★★★★★

Three days later – it was the Fourth of July weekend – lead investigating ATF agent Costelanto, his two assisting agents, and Detective Sturgis of the state police held an emergency meeting at Sturgis's office in Evansville.

"I have some good news," Costelanto announced. "Two men our agency sought for questioning have been picked up in southern France. They're the two Wyoming brothers in the videos taken here in Jefferson. Further work revealed they'd flown from Casper, Wyoming to O'Hare to London two days after Mrs. Simpson's death. From there, then flew to Geneva, then Milan, and finally, Paris. All this, in our opinion, to throw off track anyone who might have been trying to follow them. From Paris they took the high speed train to Lyon, a river boat down the Rhone to Arles and, finally, they hired someone to drive them to Aix-en-Provence where they rented an apartment. We have to give thanks to French authorities for their assistance.

"The other good news is that, although not charged, one of the pair is already talking to our agents who flew over there yesterday. We hope this leads to a major crack in the case. Extradition will not be a problem."

*****

A phone rang that night in Arlington, Virginia, shortly after 10. "Don't the fuck call me!" the voice shouted. "You don't the fuck call me. You outta your mind?"

"I had to, you gotta understand," came the frustrated reply. "I gotta know what to do. The ATF and the FBI ain't dumb. If one of those two guys starts blabbing, we're toast."

"*We're* toast? Huh! You, maybe, but not me. You hired them. You don't tie me with anything. You know the consequences of doing that. And don't ever call me again!" With that, he disconnected the call and threw the cell phone against the sofa in his apartment. "Dammit!" he screamed.

In less than 24 hours, the ATF had questions for the caller.

CHAPTER

11

As anti-incumbent movements grew across the country – some targeting state legislators and governors as well – the two leading presidential candidates were doing all they could to appease restless voters.

Everywhere Republican senator Lansing and Democratic congressman Gilford went, at rallies or in interviews, they stressed their ideas for getting both parties to work together in the future. Each said their plan would succeed. Receptions for them were lukewarm in nearly every venue except at private dinners attended by supporters.

Their parties' national conventions dripped with rhetoric.

"I recognize the frustration all of you feel," Lansing said in accepting her party's nomination in late July in Cleveland. "I, too, have been frustrated as a member of Congress. If you look at my record, *I* have tried to compromise and work across party lines, but those on the other side of the aisle have just dug in their heels. We must hold to our party's principles while continuing to work with others."

"If you elect me," Gilford stated in accepting the Democrats' nomination in Philadelphia a week later, "I promise you'll see positive action in Congress immediately. I've been a leader in attempting to get both parties to work together. The gridlock you are so deeply against will end!"

Polls showed the two neck-and-neck, with Lansing typically holding a two to three percentage point lead. Election Day was just over three months away.

★★★★★

In early October, Anthony Costelanto flew to Washington, D.C., for a meeting at the Department of Justice. Any lesser person might have been intimidated by the presence of the U.S. Attorney General, the U.S. Attorney for the Southern District of Indiana and their staffs, but not Costelanto. He was a veteran of investigations and confidently knew he possessed information for a strong case.

"We appreciate your hard work and long hours, and those of fellow agents and officers from other state and federal agencies," Attorney General Harriett Talbot stated, directing her comments to Costelanto. "The nature of what you uncovered, implicating someone in high federal service, of course, has my office involved. There is not a quiver of doubt as to whether we have jurisdiction. While there could be precedent for bringing the charges in Washington, I think they properly belong at the district level. But let's review all the facts as we know them at this point."

Costelanto summarized the key evidence. The AG, DA and their staffs talked law and possible charges.

"By wanting to intimidate Mr. Simpson, the key defendant-to-be was depriving Simpson of his civil rights," Talbot said. "Unfortunately, the intimidation led to death. We believe the brothers intended to kill Mr. Simpson. As explosives experts, they were well aware of the amount of explosive it would take to scare versus kill someone and whether to plant a device under the passenger floorboard or the driver's."

"There are other federal statutes that come into play as well," Talbot's chief deputy injected. "The brothers used interstate commerce to commit a crime, cellular phones were used in interstate travel for the commission of the crime even though murder may not have been the intent of the person who ordered the intimidation or the two under him who were involved in the hiring."

"Certainly, and there's more," Talbot responded. "Under federal law, murder is unlawful killing with malice aforethought. Again, a killing may not have been the intent of three of the persons but they're just as guilty for what transpired, especially with explosives being used. And I return to my statement that all five were involved in attempting to deny Mr. Simpson his civil right to express frustration with Congress and seek a change."

The meeting lasted more than hour. "We will continue researching the statutes," Talbot said in conclusion. "We must bring as strong a case as possible regardless of where it leads."

★★★★★

As the weeks rolled by, polls showed anticipated voter turnout to be higher than at any time in nearly half a century. National political correspondent Ed Baker reported about it on NBC Nightly News. "In the 1960s, just over sixty percent of registered voters cast ballots in presidential elections. Of course, there were major attractions then – the charismatic senator John Kennedy versus vice president Richard Nixon in 1960, the nation wanting Lyndon Johnson in 1964 instead of Barry Goldwater, and a torn nation seeking a change in 1968. But since then, turnout has been closer to 52 or 53 percent.

"Three major polling services issued their results today and on average they show an astounding 66.7 percent of voters plan to cast ballots Nov. 8. That may spell bad news for incumbents.   We asked Republican national chair Kathy Ross what she thought the significance of the results was."

"I don't view the numbers as a negative," Ross stated in the video recording. "Rather, I see them as meaning American voters have faith in their senators and representatives despite some difficult times in Congress and want to show that those in the 'anti' movements are wrong in thinking large numbers of replacements would be good for the country. I think the results on Election Day will prove the detractors wrong. People intend to vote for those who have served them well."

"Josh," Baker stated to anchor Josh Bell, "I checked with Democratic sources and while chairman Ezra Robinson was unavailable, others are troubled. Party leadership has been stressing publicly in recent weeks that it's important for incumbents to be retained, but privately, insiders are concerned the grassroots movement that began in Indiana in May is like a snowball rolling downhill – picking up speed and growing at the same time.

"Certainly, the two presidential candidates sensed this long ago and their emphasis has not been about the need to reelect those in office but rather on why *they* should be elected and what *they'd* do as president if elected. This election will be one of the most interesting in decades. Josh."

★★★★★

Four days before the elections, the U.S. Attorney General – flanked by the U.S. Attorney for the Southern District of Indiana – dropped a bombshell at a late-afternoon news conference in Washington, D.C. Charlie had been made aware of the contents at the moment the news conference began, when ATF agent Costelanto paid him a visit.

"We are today announcing the arrests of a United States Senator, his chief of staff, a resident of Baltimore, Maryland, and two residents of Wyoming in the death of Sarah Mildred Simpson of Jefferson, Indiana."

The AG continued as reporters scrawled and television cameras zoomed in.

"Senator Samuel Calhoun of Mississippi is accused of ordering an act to intimidate Mrs. Simpson's husband that resulted in death. He is charged with felony murder. His chief of staff, Michael Forrester of Arlington, Virginia, is charged with felony murder, Dominic Gerardo of Baltimore, Maryland, is charged with felony murder, and Austin Clifton and Jeremiah Clifton, of Dayton, Wyoming, are each charged with felony murder. The involvement of Senator Calhoun, Forrester, and Gerardo in this case was brought to light after the two Clifton brothers were picked up for questioning in southern France in July. A federal grand jury in the Southern District of Indiana returned the sealed indictments late this morning." Nodding toward the woman standing to her left, Attorney General Talbot said, "The U.S. attorney for the district, Wanda Pollack, will try the cases. All five of the defendants are in federal custody here in Washington.

"We want to thank the Bureau of Alcohol, Tobacco, Firearms, and Explosives for leading the investigation but also the Federal Bureau of Investigation, Indiana state police and local authorities in Indiana for their unwavering support and involvement."

Talbot revealed little information other than to say Senator Calhoun, elected as an Independent in 2004, was in a close race for his seat in the 2016 election, and feared the anti-incumbent campaign would take him under. Several rallies denouncing incumbents had been held in Mississippi.

"While Senator Calhoun had received substantial monetary support from lobbyists during his nearly twelve years in office," Talbot stated, "there is no evidence that his criminal act was tied to any higher authority or organization. We have ruled out any link to terrorism. We believe he acted alone, except for those who were responsible under him. Our investigation will continue and other charges may follow."

Under questioning, Talbot revealed all five had been arrested without incident, including the final three at their homes that morning. She also said that even if the senator did not order the actual killing of the victim, he was still responsible for a felony that led to murder. A request for capital punishment of all five, she said, is being considered.

The news lit up Facebook, Twitter, and the regular news media like a high-noon cloudless summer sun.

Angry social media enthusiasts called for the defeat of every congressman and senator seeking reelection regardless of who they were and what position they held in leadership.

The arrests were the lead story on every national network newscast that evening. CBS Evening News correspondent Bob Lensing's coverage was typical. "The news of a U.S. Senator accused of orchestrating a plan that resulted in a woman's death has sent shock waves throughout Capitol Hill. My experience is that Senator Calhoun was respected by most members of Congress, although he didn't hold a leadership position on any of the three committees in which he served.

"Senators and representatives of both the Democratic and Republican parties, and the two presidential nominees, immediately began distancing themselves from Calhoun, most calling his alleged act 'despicable' or 'unconscionable.' The party chairs said their men and women in Congress serve with the highest ethics and morals and do all they can to represent their constituents well, and they knew everyone stood united in believing that no matter what the challenges of working across party lines, there is no excuse to harm another person.

"Calhoun's attorney said his client was innocent and the government had a flawed case that in no way implicates the senator.

"We'll see. With the election only four days away, the mood of the country has plenty of time to react and the betting among everyone I have talked with here in Washington is that attitudes toward incumbents may be in a free fall."

★★★★★

As soon as his brief meeting with ATF agent Costelanto had ended, Charlie left the store and went home and closed all the blinds and drapes in his house. He would be besieged by media. He took his land line phone off the hook. Friends could call his cell if they wanted.

Just after 5 o'clock, Dick Jones called from the store to say national networks and correspondents from major newspapers were there begging to talk with him. Charlie refused. "Tell them I have no comment and you have no idea where I am. For your information, I'll open at the regular time tomorrow. If the media won't leave you alone, call Chief Miles."

It wasn't long before a steady stream of knocks on his front, side, and back doors and voices calling out "Mr. Simpson, are you home?" began. Charlie had disconnected the doorbell weeks earlier. Sitting in his Lazy Boy recliner, his sock-covered feet propped on the foot rest and the TV volume turned low, he smiled – a big smile – at the thought of the media outside, unable to get to him, but especially at the knowledge that the bastards who killed Sarah were behind bars. He hoped they all would get the death penalty.

★★★★★

On advice of the ATF, Charlie refused to answer questions when confronted by the media the following morning. They tried to talk to him when he walked from his house to the car in the driveway. They were waiting at the store when he arrived at the rear and parked the vehicle. "I'm sorry but on legal advice, I cannot say anything," Charlie answered over and over while holding his arms up and motioning with his open hands as he walked to the back door, unlocked it, and closed it behind him. It was an hour before the store's 9 a.m. opening time.

But the media would not leave. Sitting in his office, he stewed. Finally, at 8:50, he went to the front door, opened it, and addressed the collection of reporters, cameramen and photographers.

"Thank you for your interest. As I said a little while ago, I cannot discuss the case, on advice of the ATF and government attorneys. I will do nothing to undermine it.

"That being said, I'm extremely pleased and relieved that arrests have been made and I look forward to justice being carried out." He took a long pause. "I've always tried being cooperative with you but I will ask that you cooperate with me and not come into the store and disrupt my business. *Please.*"

Charlie hadn't turned before questions came from every direction from the fifty or so media assembled on the sidewalk and the edge of the street. He couldn't resist one.

"What about the anti-Congress campaign, Mr. Simpson? What do you say to Americans?"

Charlie stopped. "The greatest gift the country could give itself would be a fresh set of legislators in Washington."

He walked back into the store, leaving reporters to continue yelling questions. He turned on the neon OPEN sign. None of the media entered.

CHAPTER
12

Journalists reported throughout Nov. 8 that the Election Day turnout was unlike anything in modern times.

"I've been working the polls for almost forty years and there's never been early-morning voting like I saw today," the polling judge stated to Fox News in Burlington, Vermont. "There's been a steady stream of voters the entire day," said another in Sheridan, Wyoming. Fox Correspondent Martha Thompson reported the atmosphere at some polls around the country to be jubilant, while at others the faces of voters in line appeared stern, as though on a mission. "Expect something we've never seen after the counting begins," Thompson predicted.

Charlie had closed the store for the day, placing a hand-scrawled "Closed for Election Day" sign next to the "Clean House (and Senate)" sign on the front and back doors. He knew he'd be besieged by reporters if he tried to stay open, so the easiest – yet costly – thing to do was to close.

After voting at his polling place in Thomas Jefferson Elementary School and talking fifteen minutes with reporters who met him outside afterward, Charlie drove to other polling sites in the town and then to Pemberton, where he observed long lines at every location he passed. *My God, it's worked,* he thought as he hit his closed fist onto the steering wheel.

Parking his car two blocks from his house, Charlie weaved and jogged through neighbors' yards to his back door, eluding media in the street in front of the house, then spent the afternoon on his computer in the small study, reading reports from various internet sites about voter turnout, reaction, and predictions throughout the nation. He could hear CNN coverage on this television in the living room, his heartbeat increasing as he moved from website to website, getting more and more excited about the reality he'd dreamed of.

Seldom drinking anything but wine, and that sporadically, Charlie poured bourbon on ice and took a long sip just before the polls closed in the eastern U.S. It was 5 p.m. in Jefferson, located in a small pocket of southwestern Indiana in the Central time zone. Charlie wished he could have Mary Carnahan with him. Mary'd been loyal in joining him, Jason, and Jack in launching their campaign and sticking with it. He knew that as a widow with no family in the area, she was likely spending the evening alone, but he wouldn't call. His interest had no connection to romance; he just wanted to share the evening with someone. But if people found out he and Mary had been alone in his house, only five months after Sarah died, there'd be a flurry of gossip.

He had his choice of channels and started with CBS Evening News which began its 6 p.m. EST election coverage with projections of three representatives' and one senator's losses. Anchor Fred Cunningham began the broadcast, "Perhaps this is just the tip of the iceberg that may be moving through the national political landscape tonight. CBS News projects Democrat Toby Wheeler, a two-term congressman from Vermont, Representative Claudia Johnson, Democrat from New York, who's served nearly eight years, influential Republican congressman Will Myers of Florida – twelve years in the House, and Senator Todd Smith, a Delaware Republican serving two terms, will lose their seats to their opponents. Numerous other races are simply too close to call."

Charlie hit the remote's DOWN channel button and joined NBC Nightly News. Anchor Josh Bell was in the midst of his opening report. "In summary, it already appears that at least four incumbent U.S. senators will be defeated and at least a dozen representatives. The biggest name thus far is Representative Will Myers, a Florida Republican, chairman of the powerful House Judiciary Committee. Hang onto your seats, folks, this night might get very interesting."

ABC News' national political correspondent Tonya Bayliss was at her large map of the U.S., using electronics to show states where colors were switched from red to blue and vice versa, representing changes the network was projecting as the results came in. "To think, these five senators and sixteen representatives who we believe have been defeated are only from those states where the polls have closed. We still have three more time zones to go. By 9 or 9:30 tonight, Eastern time, the results could be staggering. Nothing like this has ever happened in a United States election.

"Among those we predict have lost their seats are House Minority Whip Dennis Tempel of New Hampshire, Will Myers, chairman of the Judiciary Committee in the House – now in his sixth term from Florida, and House Veterans Affairs chairman David Sellers, a Republican. What is really surprising about this one is that Sellers is a Vietnam veteran and has been in office fourteen years, six of them as chair. On the Senate side, it appears Democratic Policy Committee chair Barbara Keith of North Carolina will lose, while three-term Republican John David Snider of Alabama, chair of the Transportation Committee, is in the fight of his life.

"Oh, there's one other. It's a coincidence but as we think about what became a national anti-incumbent movement and it being started by a handful of small-business owners in Indiana, perhaps it is only fitting that the chairman of the House Small Business Committee, Sherman Tucker, a Democrat from eastern Kentucky, has lost his reelection bid."

Every network Charlie watched – CNN, Fox, MSNBC – was abuzz with the climactic changes taking place. The rapidly incoming results and predictions were fodder for the latter two with their left and right-leaning analysts. Harrison Boyer on Fox News was aghast that so many experienced conservatives were being voted out in favor of liberals whom he felt "would change the course of the nation certainly not for the good." Opposing commentator Sylvia Sullivan rebutted that "the loss of key liberal leaders would not be good for the country but for completely different reasons. The very thought that……." Charlie changed channels.

Nearly forgotten in the opening minutes of the broadcasts was the presidential race. Early results showed Lansing and Gifford locked in a close contest with no network venturing to make a call as to which would win. CBS' Cunningham said, "Based on what we've seen thus far, this could be a long evening for both candidates. I hope they got some good rest last night."

Charlie was nearly shaking, the drink glass almost empty when he called Jack Peterson. "Jack, Charlie. You watching TV?"

"My God, am I!" Peterson exclaimed. "Charlie, this could be an explosive night. Hang on, bud." Charlie could hear the glee.

Charlie poured another bourbon and added ice. This time with a splash of water.

Back at CBS, he heard national political analyst Gloria Alvarez state, "The national elections are not the only ones being impacted by the voters' obvious ire. Of course, opinion polls showed over and over a disdain for the congressional gridlock. What we didn't know for certain were opinions about legislators in the states. And from what we've seen in early results from state after state, the anti-incumbent attitude carried over. And none of it is confined to one party versus the other.

"In fact, exit polls from throughout the country today showed many voters didn't care about party affiliation, the length of time a person had been in office, or the position they held.

"On the other hand, there are some House districts where registered voters are so heavily Republican or Democratic that it's likely those congressmen and women will be retained in office. In fact, some already have."

As the hours went by, polls closed, and results continued coming in, the stunning changes ahead in Congress became more and more evident.

ABC News was the first to declare a major loss. Anchor Martha Williams: "Here is a shocker. Not a shock that we're predicting it but a shock by who it is. ABC News projects that Senate President Pro Tem Martin Monahan of Florida has lost his reelection bid after twenty-four years in the upper chamber. Monahan's position places him fourth in line for the presidency of our country, behind the president, vice president, and speaker of the House. This is really stunning."

"And, Martha," Tonya Bayliss broke in, "we want to remind voters in the far west that polls will be open nearly thirty minutes more, so they shouldn't assume everything is over. It's far from it."

Over the next three hours, networks reported incredulous results unlike any in history.

About midnight, Charlie, worn out from elation-induced tension and two drinks, fell asleep in his recliner. He awoke to the ringing of his cell phone and the sound from his TV. His head throbbed. "Charlie, can you believe it? Can you believe what has happened to America?" a jubilant Mary Carnahan exclaimed into the phone as he tried to make sense of what was being said. He mumbled in reply. "Been asleep since, uh, midnight, so haven't heard anything." He looked at the clock sitting on top of the television. It was 6:07 a.m. "We did it, Charlie. We did it. Just turn on any channel and you'll be astounded. Oh, my God, Charlie, we did it."

Still in his recliner, he reached for the remote that had fallen to the floor beside him, turned up the sound, and over the next half hour heard the results: An unprecedented seventy-three percent voter turnout. The presidential race was still too close to call. Lansing was slightly ahead in the popular vote but Gilford held an advantage in the electoral totals. The results in four states were already being contested by charges of fraud, ghost voters, and intimidation.

Bleary-eyed ABC News Anchor Williams summarized the election: "It's been a long night and many of us are tired, but we've witnessed an historic political hurricane. An astounding 197 incumbents in the House of Representatives – forty-five percent – have been voted out of office, and an equally astonishing number – 20 – of the senators who were up for reelection, have been dismissed. The list of leadership positions that will change reads like a Who's Who. House Speaker David Flores of Texas has apparently been reelected but his opponent is already demanding a recount. Overall, the balance of power between the Democrats and Republicans in the two houses has not changed much.

"Here's who have been voted out of office.

"In the Senate, the president pro tem, the Republican majority leader, the Democratic conference committee chair, the policy committee chairs of both parties, and the chairs of these committees – appropriations, finance, and foreign relations.

"In the House, the majority and minority leaders, the minority whip, the Democratic caucus chair, and the Republican conference chair, plus the chairs of the armed services, foreign affairs, judiciary, small business, veterans affairs and ways and means committees.

"These are powerful positions in Congress and they will have new leadership come January. Amazing. Shocking. Unbelievable. Whatever adjective you want to place on it, nothing can correctly describe what has happened. One thing we know, however, is America will change."

Representation in Congress had changed in a resounding way. Constituents voiced their opinions prior to the elections. Politicians had not believed the messages strongly enough and paid the price. They included Charlie's congressman Wilburn with whom he finally met in August.

Anchor Williams had one more. "Independent Senator Samuel Calhoun, in jail for the June death of an Indiana woman – a tragedy that seemed to propel the 'anti' movement – had Mississippi voters turn out in massive numbers against him. He was beaten soundly."

Charlie stretched in the recliner and smiled. Then he thought of Sarah. The smile disappeared.

He hoped America would be different, led by fresh faces, ideas, and willingness to compromise in Congress. *But was it worth it?* he allowed himself to wonder. He – Sarah – had paid a terrible price for what he believed and fought for. Life without her would be difficult.

He cried.

Then sitting in silence, Charlie pondered, *What about eliminating, or at least overhauling, the political parties?*

The grandfather clock chimed.

It was time to go to work.